MAC WAL

AMERICAN
(Mac Walke. .. .,

Sequel to MAC WALKER'S 40,000 FEET

D.W. Ulsterman

OTHER NOVELS BY D.W. ULSTERMAN

MAC WALKER'S 40,000 FEET
(Mac Walker #1)

MAC WALKER'S BENGHAZI
(Mac Walker #3)

MAC WALKER'S BETRAYAL
(Mac Walker #4)

DOMINATUS
(Mac Walker #5)

TUMULTUS
(Mac Walker #6)

THE SECOND OLDEST PROFESSION **– FREE!!**
(Bennington #1)

BENNINGTON P.I. "Bonita"
(Bennington #2)

BENNINGTON P.I. "Take two and call me in the morgue"
(Bennington #3)

BENNINGTON P.I. Illuminati
(Bennington #4)

http://ulstermanbooks.com/

Dedicated to my older brother**

A father, a son, a brother, a friend,

and a Marine combat veteran.

He left much too soon…

R.I.P.

"It's a hell of a thing, killing a man.
Take away all he's got and all he's ever gonna have."

-Unforgiven

Prologue:

April 21st, 2004

Hamid Gilani had been killing men, women, and children not necessarily because he enjoyed doing so, but that he was quite good at it. He recalled very few of the faces and even fewer of the names. Those who died were no more than passing casualties for a much greater cause and his was the blessed hand to deliver God's justice upon this earth. Lives were meaningless in a world torn asunder by moral corruption.

So...let them taste part of what they have done that perhaps they will return to righteousness.

It was a quote from the Koran Hamid repeated often. Humankind must be returned to righteousness, and he would be a great soldier to pave the necessary path for that return.

The detonation just outside the Riyadh national police headquarters was considerable, promising the great blessings of death and injury to the many caught in the blast, including if all went as planned, the death of the American Deputy Secretary of State who was to be using the facility for a meeting with the Saudi Foreign Minister.

Hamid watched the explosion and the resulting panic from the top of a business district building some five hundred yards away. The car was stocked with ten pounds of a simple Semtex that had originated from a trusted Indonesian supplier. The family of the vehicle's driver was given a hundred thousand Saudi Riyads for their oldest son's willingness to sacrifice himself for what was described to them as "Allah's will." Such participants were legion throughout the world, yet another sign Hamid took as confirming his work was in fact blessed by God Himself.

It took several minutes for the smoke to dissipate enough to allow Hamid to get a better look at the damage. Nearly the entire front of the police barracks was blown apart with only remnants of the former fortified structure remaining. Hamid smiled at the sound of shrieking sirens as security forces began to respond to the chaos.

Praise Allah, this is a great success!

His phone was ringing. Only one other knew the number – Ramtin Armeen, Hamid's longtime benefactor and primary investor in their shared goal of bringing the sinful tyranny of Western Civilization to an end.

"You failed."

Ramtin's low voice made clear his dissatisfaction. Hamid lifted his binoculars to his eyes once again and surveyed the damage below.

"No, it is done. I am watching it now."

There was a long pause before Ramtin continued.

"The American politician was not yet there. The original meeting time was delayed by thirty minutes. The most important aspect of the operation failed, thus *you* failed as well. Return to the safe house for pick up. Transport will arrive within the hour. I have another job for you. It is time we activate the cells. Today's failure indicates our work is being too closely monitored. Let us expedite counter measures. Understood?"

Hamid nodded to himself as he watched several Saudi emergency response vehicles begin to set up a perimeter around the just destroyed police barracks.

"Yes, understood."

The call was ended.

Hamid looked up at the deep blue Saudi Arabian sky. The late morning temperature was already nearing ninety degrees. He was going to miss Riyadh. It was truly among the most beautiful cities on earth, a fascinating blend of old and new and filled with some of the most wonderfully vibrant people.

Duty called though, as it always did. God's work did not rest.

It was time to return to America.

1.

February 5th, 2005

Mac Walker sat alone in the small waiting room of a strip mall dentist office off of Columbia Pike some twenty minutes outside of Washington D.C.

The attractive blonde female receptionist offered him a reassuring smile. She was in her late-twenties and likely armed. Mac began to silently wonder what sidearm she might be carrying. He guessed her to be ex-military like himself, possibly even a Marine. She appeared no more than five foot six, medium build, and right-handed. Her hands were smallish, so the former Navy SEAL assumed that would rule out the Glock 42.

Bet she has the SIG P239, a sexy weapon for a sexy woman.

Mac peered out through the thick window glass that overlooked the compacted gravel parking area that ran the length of the small strip mall. He could tell the glass was actually one inch bullet resistant Polycarbonate. The gravel would make it difficult for a vehicle or even someone on foot to arrive at the location without making noise. The dentist office was at the end of the mall's right side. There were only three other office spaces and all of them appeared to be vacant. With the building located some seventy yards off the road, it gave a wide view of anyone approaching. From a military standpoint it wasn't a bad location for a covert meeting – remote enough for privacy, yet also hiding in plain sight and reasonably built to withstand an attack.

"Sir, they're ready to see you."

Mac stood up and began moving toward the office door located to the left of the reception desk. Before opening it he paused to look back at the blonde behind the desk.

"SIG P239, am I right?"

The woman's brow furrowed as she cocked her head to the left.

"I'm sorry, what did you say?"

"Your sidearm, is it the SIG?"

The blonde's eyes widened just slightly and then she gave Mac a quick half smile.

"You better hope to never find out, sir."

Mac chuckled. The woman had a personality as attractive as her looks. He opened the door and was only mildly surprised to find a vast and well lit open interior that occupied the entirety of the strip mall structure. In the center of the room was found a long conference table and eight matching black leather chairs. Two of those chairs were currently occupied.

The first man was Ray Tilley, Mac's Project Icon operations supervisor. Tilley provided the assignments and the payment for a job well done. He was the one who had initially recruited Mac for the covert military program after a crazy plane ride back from Paris a few years earlier. Mac considered Tilley to be a good man and just as important, he paid on time every time.

Ray Tilley rose from his chair looking genuinely pleased to be once again seeing Mac in person. Tilley was middle aged, of average build and height, and politically well connected. Mac glanced at the older, silver-haired second man, trying to place the familiar face.

"Mac, allow me to introduce you to Senator Jackson Elder. Senator, this is our assignment leader for Project Icon, Mr. Mac Walker."

The senator remained seated, his eyes watching Mac closely as he approached the table. Mac nodded while his mind quickly recalled what he knew of the powerful North Dakota senator.

Sixty-two years old, halfway through his third term, chairs the Senate Intelligence Committee, and served two tours with the Army in Vietnam back in the day as a helicopter pilot. That means he's seen some shit. The average lifespan for a chopper pilot in that war was just over a month.

"Mr. Tilley, I assume your man here understands this meeting right now isn't actually taking place?"

Tilley motioned for Mac to take a seat and then did the same.

"Of course, Senator, this is off the books. That's how we always operate."

Senator Elder's thin lipped mouth curled downward into a pronounced frown as he continued to glare at Mac.

"This thing isn't just off the books, Mr. Tilley. This here *never happened*. I'm not here, none of us are here."

Ray tried to keep the appearance of assured calm, though internally he was growing annoyed by the senator's persistent concern. This wasn't his first rodeo.

"As I said, Senator, this is how we operate. You've reviewed Mr. Walker's file, Project Icon's work, there's no need to worry over confidentiality or our absolute discretion."

The senator's right hand moved up to his long, Romanesque nose and proceeded to seemingly dig for gold while his eyes left Mac to look over at Tilley.

"Ok then, let's get this thing done. Tell me if he's in or out, so I can get back to D.C."

"Ray, I got the call and flew up here ASAP like you asked. Maybe you should tell me what this is about so we can get the senator back to doing all that important work senators do, like banging interns, spending our tax dollars, and breaking all those promises that got them elected."

Tilley winced, awaiting the angry retort he was certain to come from the senator. Instead he was stunned to find the Army veteran shaking his head and then laughing.

"I was told you were an even bigger asshole than I am! Ok then, Mr. Tilley, do like the man asked. Tell him why the hell we're sitting here staring at one another."

Ray reached under the desk and retrieved a metallic briefcase which he then placed on the table and opened. He withdrew three manila folders, giving one each to Mac and the senator, and leaving one for himself.

Mac was amused by the old-school approach.

"This kind of feels like something out of the 1950's - briefcases, folders...no computer print outs for this one, huh?"

Tilley closed the briefcase and opened his folder while the senator leaned over the table and pointed at Mac.

"That's right, no computers. That shit is *always* traceable. I like old-school, Mr. Walker, so this is how we do it. If people knew even half of what we were doing with just their phones I bet a lot more others would be going old-school too. Either that, or they'd be stringing this government up by its balls."

Mac shrugged.

"I can't do anything but agree with everything you just said, Senator. By all means, Ray, proceed."

Tilley cleared his throat and then did just that.

"If you open your file, gentlemen, you'll first come to a photograph."

Mac looked down at the image of a handsome, youngish, dark skinned man staring back at him while Tilley continued with the briefing.

"This is Ramtin Armeen, aged thirty-nine. He's an Iranian born, Harvard educated businessman who seven years ago inherited Melli Corporation from his father, a large multi-national with offices throughout the world, though he works primarily out of Chicago, New York, London, and of course, Tehran. His current net worth is estimated to be just over nine billion dollars."

Mac let out a low whistle while Senator Elder looked like he wanted to tear his copy of the photograph apart.

"Yeah, he's a rich, sick son-of-a-bitch for sure. I've been told he's Bin Laden on steroids."

Mac looked up at the senator while pointing to his own copy of the photograph.

"This guy?"

Senator Elder nodded as the left side of his mouth curled into a snarl.

"Hell yeah *that guy*. Bin Laden had at most maybe fifty million of his own money and look how much shit he rained down on us. This guy is likely just as radical, but he's got a hell of a lot more than fifty million to go after us with."

Tilley looked at Mac and nodded his agreement with the senator.

"Ramtin Armeen might be the most dangerous man in the world right now, Mac. Not just because he's a billionaire militant, but he's also smart. He keeps himself two steps ahead of us. When we thought we were getting close, he left New York for London, then shortly after that he was in Madrid, and then Paris, and finally he ended up in Tehran for six months until our leads went cold - until six weeks ago. He's back in the United States, but all his communications have gone silent. It's as if he's not talking to anyone. No phone messages, no emails, as far as surveillance goes he's a living breathing ghost."

The senator let out a long, disgusted sigh.

"We know he's got something planned, something *big*, we just don't know exactly what."

"How do you know that, Senator? And if you do, why not just pick this guy up, hold him for questioning and go all Patriot Act on his ass?"

The senator looked to Tilley to answer for him. Ray pulled out the second page from the file.

"This is an excerpt from a CIA interrogation from three months earlier. The subject was a twenty-six year old male who was picked up trying to enter Canada at Vancouver International Airport. He was arriving from Malaysia. Before Malaysia he had spent nine days in Madrid Spain and then left there less than twenty four hours before the train bombings that killed 191 people. He has ties to Iraqi militants, as well as another radical Islamic group in Malaysia. They were the ones attempting to get him to a safe house in Vancouver when Canadian authorities flagged his entry and then handed him over to us. Take a moment to read the excerpt, Mac."

SUBJECT: I had nothing to do with the train bombings! I had nothing to do with any of it! I heard rumors, you know, talking, but that is it!

Int. #1: Then why did you leave Madrid 24hrs prior to the attack?

SUBJECT: I was coming home. It was a vacation and I was coming home. I have nothing to say about the train bombings. I don't know anything. You can't hold me here like this."

Int. #1: What was your purpose in attempting to enter Canada?

SUBJECT: To see friends.

Int. #1: Who?

SUBJECT: Just friends. That is my business.

Int. #2: What is your relationship with Al-Zarqawi in Iraq?

SUBJECT: Nothing, I don't know who you're talking about.

Subject shown 2004 photograph with subject meeting with Al-Zarqawi

Int. #2: You don't? Isn't this you meeting with him last year?

Subject doesn't answer.

Int.#1: We can give you protection, but you have to cooperate.

Subject says nothing.

Subject shown 2004 photograph with subject meeting with unknown man in Madrid three days prior to April 2004 train bombing.

Int. #1: Who is this man you met with in Madrid?
Subject looks at photo/says nothing.

Int. #2: Show him the other photograph. His family.

Subject shown photograph of two young children

Int. #1: Are those your children? They are waiting for you in Malaysia, right? Would you like to see them again?

Subject says nothing.

Int. #2: When you didn't show in Vancouver, you think that might have spooked some of your associates? You think they might not get concerned? Maybe decide to do what needs to be done to keep everyone else quiet? There were nearly 200 killed in Madrid. What are a couple more kids hiding out in Malaysia, right? We can help keep them safe though if you just cooperate with us. Who is the man you met with in Madrid?

Subject looks at photograph.

SUBJECT: You promise to keep him away from my family? To keep my children safe?

Int. #1: Yes, we will do our best to keep your family safe, but we're running out of time.

SUBJECT: His name is Hamid.

Int. #2: Hamid what?

SUBJECT: That is all I know – Hamid.

Int. #2: Is this Hamid connected to the train bombing in Madrid?

SUBJECT: I don't know. I am speaking the truth. I don't know that for certain.

Int. #1: But you believe he might have been – this Hamid?

Subject nods in the affirmative

Int. #1: Do you know where we can find this Hamid now?

Question is repeated

SUBJECT: He could be anywhere. I do know...

Subject pauses

SUBJECT: I do know he speaks very good English.

Int. #2: Is he American?

SUBJECT: He speaks very good English.

Int. #1: You need to tell us more than that. You think he is here, in the United States? Is that correct?

Subject nods in the affirmative

Int. #2: Where the hell is he? Why is he here? Are you planning another Madrid style attack in the United States?

Subject says nothing

Int. #2: I'm tired of this shit. Let our Malaysian resources know they can stand down. If this guy wants his family dead by morning, I don't care.

Int. #1: Is that what you want to happen? Are you willing to let your children die to keep this Hamid safe?

Subject sighs loudly

Int. #2: This is bullshit. He doesn't know anything. I'm making the call to Malaysia. We're wasting our time here.

Int. #1: Yeah, I guess you're right. Call Malaysia.

Subject becomes visibly agitated

SUBJECT: Wait! Please, I have told you what I know. Yes, I believe he is in the United States. It is said he can come and go without surveillance. He is a citizen, an American citizen. And he always has money, lots of it.

Int. #1: Is he planning an attack in the United States?

SUBJECT: I don't know.

Subject pauses

SUBJECT: I don't know, but I think it is possible, yes. I was told, not by Hamid, but another in Malaysia, I was told Madrid was just a test.

Int. #2: A test for what?

Subject shrugs

SUBJECT: Something bigger, that is all I was told. And I believe…

Int. #1: Yes, what is it? What do you believe?

SUBJECT: I believe it will be here, in America. Yes, that there is an attack being planned in your country.

END INTERROGATION EXCERPT.

Mac looked up at Tilley and then to the senator.

"This is a lot of talking, but it don't really say all that much."

Senator Elder pointed to the folder in front of Mac.

"Look at the next photograph."

Mac pulled out a black and white photo of a burnt out late model automobile date stamped as being taken seventeen days earlier.

'That there is a vehicle that was being driven by the same young man interviewed by our CIA three months ago. The same fella that indicated he believed this Hamid is planning something big right here inside of America. Maybe another September 11th, or maybe something even worse. The body was charred up good, but we got a DNA confirmation. His name was Yong Mujumdar. Born in Malaysia and drafted into an Islamic militant group there about ten years ago. A sad, stupid little son-of-a-bitch."

Mac peered back down at the charred remains of the vehicle.

"What about his family? Did we keep them safe like we promised?"

The senator gave an indifferent grunt.

"Hell if I know, why?"

The former Navy SEAL easily matched the intensity of the senator's gaze.

"Because we promised we would, that's why."

Tilley quickly interjected, familiar with Mac's sense of honor and his just as dedicated negative outlook on most things politically related - particularly politicians themselves.

"I believe they are doing fine, Mac. Whatever measures taken to silence Mr. Mujumdar appear to have ended with his own death."

Mac leaned his head back against his shoulders and then rolled it from right to left, attempting to work out the stiffness invading his neck and shoulders while Tilley continued with the briefing.

"Just days prior to the discovery of Mujumdar's burnt remains being found inside that car, U.S. intelligence was suddenly digesting several reports of chatter regarding an impending attack inside the United States. Most concerning was that this chatter was originating from multiple locations all over the country. New York, Chicago, Seattle, Los Angeles, Houston, San Diego, Atlanta, Memphis, Boston, Baltimore, Phoenix, Minneapolis, Cleveland, even Honolulu. The chatter was all very similar, culminating within the same time frame, and then it went silent. Like a switch was turned off. I'm not talking the chatter diminished, Mac. I'm telling you it was there, and then it was gone. Like *that*."

Tilley snapped his fingers to emphasize how quickly the chatter ceased. Mac already knew the answer as to why.

"Someone ordered them to go silent. You think it's this Hamid he spoke of during the interrogation?"

The senator withdrew a third photograph from his packet and waited for Mac and Tilley to do the same. Tilley nodded at Mac.

"Yes, what you have in front of you now are two images of Hamid Gilani, one with a full beard and one without. It took us several weeks to confirm his identity. Current age is forty-five, born in Chicago to an American mother and a father from Afghanistan. We believe Hamid travelled to Afghanistan in the 1980's to fight for the Taliban against the Soviets. During his time there he trained with militants directly linked to Bin Laden where he acquired a reputation for being something of a badass. Our own CIA records claim he personally took out at least twenty Soviet soldiers in less than a year. And we would know since we were helping to arm him and the other Taliban he was running with. Eventually he made his way back to the United States, rented a small studio apartment in New York City in 1999. He remained in New York until moving back to Chicago in August of 2001. We have been unable to determine how he paid for his apartment, food, clothing etc. during his time in New York. He was interviewed twice in Chicago by the FBI after 9-11, but gave us nothing to confirm any links he might have had to the terrorist attacks on that day."

The senator snorted.

"Which is bullshit of course, our boys knew he was involved somehow, they just didn't have the information to prove it. Plus, he was lawyered up real good the second time they questioned him. Some big shot Muslim Brotherhood attorney. That was a bit of a mistake on their part though, because that brought Ramtin Armeen to our attention. He's the one giving Hamid the orders. We're pretty certain that's who paid for the attorney, the New York apartment…everything."

Mac looked back at the photograph of Ramtin Armeen.
"So Ramtin was the one who actually ordered whatever group was responsible for the chatter to go silent, right? He tells Hamid and Hamid tells everyone else."

Senator Elder nodded.

"Yes sir, that's how we see it."

Tilley looked at Mac and then spoke in a tone that made it clear how serious the situation really was.

"It also means they've gone operational, Mac. We could be just weeks, maybe even days out from them pulling the pin on this thing. CIA thinks there are at least twelve terror cells involved, spread out in major cities all over the country, but we don't have enough to move against them. We're just watching and waiting and I think that's exactly what Ramtin Armeen is counting on. They might have been planning this for years, so they don't need to communicate anymore. The order went out, and now they're ready to go. It could be hundreds dead, thousands, tens of thousands…who knows?"

The senator shifted in his chair as he glared down at the photos in front of him.

"It's a goddamn Jihad they have planned. That's all these people know. It's all they understand, and I sure as hell ain't gonna sit on my ass and just let them get away with it!"

The senator's hand slammed the top of the table and then he pointed at Mac.

"Tilley here tells me you're the very best he's got, Mr. Walker. I've seen your military file. I reviewed the report of what you did saving all those people in that hijacked airliner. You've been shot, stabbed, beat to shit, but you seem to have a rather amazing and admirable knack for not only surviving, but more importantly, getting back up and finishing the job."

Mac sat silent for a moment and then slowly folded his hands in front of him.

"What's the job, Senator?"

Tilley was prepared to answer, but was quickly cut off by Senator Elder.

"The job is you going out there and cutting off the two main heads of this very dangerous snake, Mr. Walker. I don't much care how you do it, just so long as it gets done, and gets done *quick*. We have you send both those terrorist bastards to the hell they so richly deserve. I think the rest of them will stand down. It'll scare the shit out of them…give us more time to gather evidence and then bring them all in. They want to do some Jihad on *us*? Well okay then, we're gonna unleash you to give them a taste of their own medicine. You deliver them an *American Jihad*, Mr. Walker. I want you to take those sons-a-bitches OUT."

Mac looked across the table at Ray Tilley.

"What's it pay?"

Tilley gave a quick half smile, knowing that once Mac asked about price that meant he had most likely decided to take the assignment.

"Fifty thousand cash up front, and a hundred thousand after both targets are terminated. I already have a safe house ready to go, alternate identification, passports, weapons, everything you need, Mac."

Mac's eyebrows rose slightly. A hundred and fifty thousand was a significant payoff.

"No-one else from the team on this – just me?"

Tilley nodded.

"This isn't even a Project Icon assignment. This is so far off the books…you'd be a lone wolf. No help from anyone. All funds in non-traceable cash, same with the weapons, your identification, the safe house, everything."

Mac *was* interested, but not yet entirely sold. He had never been given an assignment inside the United States. Such things were generally frowned upon in his line of work – too many potential complications.

"Why me? Why hasn't CIA, Homeland Security, or the FBI taken this on?"

Senator Elder cursed under his breath and then slid another photograph toward Mac.

"Take a look. You know what that is?"

Mac glanced down then looked back down again, uncertain he was actually seeing what he thought.

"That, Senator, appears to be a small pile of shit."

Tilley cleared his throat.

"That's exactly what it is, Mr. Walker. Pig shit to be precise. It was sent to CIA headquarters in Langley last month. Just a simple box and a pile of shit in a plastic bag with the name of a CIA agent printed on the outside. That agent had been tracking Hamid Gilani for several months. Then she disappeared. Then this box shows up. CIA did a DNA test and determined a match."

Even Mac Walker, who had seen plenty of horror in his still relatively young life, found himself shocked at the story Tilley was telling him. The senator's voice bellowed his own disgust at the photograph.

"Yeah, they killed our agent and fed her to some goddamn pigs! Or worse, she might have been eaten alive. Apparently these people won't eat pork, but they sure as hell have no problem feeding a human being to them. Now tell him about the schools, Mr. Tilley."

Ray Tilley straightened in his chair and paused for a moment before continuing.

"Toward the end of the chatter phase, the names and locations of several schools were mentioned. No specific threats, but a long list of school facilities ranging from college campuses to daycare centers, East Coast, West Coast, and various locations in between. Another school name was repeated as well, several times – Beslan."

Mac leaned forward as his eyes narrowed.

"Beslan? As in the Beslan Massacre?"

Tilley nodded.

The Beslan Massacre had been a horrific terrorist attack upon a large school in the town of Beslan, Russia. Children, parents, and teachers were taken hostage for three days by Muslim militants. Three hundred and sixty-six people were killed, nearly half of which were children.

"These people already confirmed how sick and twisted they are when they sent us our agent back in a box of pig shit. They sure as hell will have no problem blowing up a bunch of schools. And if they coordinate this to happen on the same day, all across the country…"

The senator's voice trailed off into silence.

"Do you think Armeen had something to do with Beslan? Why would an Iranian-born militant be linked to Islamic separatists in Russia?"

Tilley shrugged at Mac's question.

"We don't know for certain, but a man with the kind of resources Ramtin Armeen has, billions of dollars, that could buy a lot of blood, Mac. There are people in this world willing to blow themselves up for a lot less. What I can tell you is this – I've reviewed the data, the contacts, the links, the past history and the current threats of both Armeen and Gilani. These are two very-very bad players in the War on Terror. They have something planned, something terrible, and it's gonna happen soon if we don't take them out."

The senator's heavily knuckled right pointer finger jabbed the top of the conference table hard enough the sound echoed against the walls of the room.

"Mr. Walker, this operation has the support of some people very high up in this nation's political food chain, understood? There are to be *no* lawyers, *no* trial publicity, *no* martyrdom for these bastards. We simply want them dead and gone and if you are able to do that for us, this nation will be in your debt."

Mac Walker looked from the senator to Tilley and then nodded once.

"Ok, I'm in."

2.

24 hours later...

Mac parked his rented black four-door sedan down a narrow alley in the bustling Chicago Chinatown district, home to an Asian community that numbered nearly seventy thousand and was as self contained a neighborhood as one could find in the city.

It was also, according to Tilley, a good place to hide out.

Mac's safe house was a second floor studio just above a vacant commercial property. Because no business was currently occupying the space below he was allowed to park his vehicle next to the narrow steel framed stairway to the apartment. The door was half-inch thick reinforced steel and housed in an equally heavy steel frame and secured by two deep bolt locks. If somebody wished to break in it would prove both difficult and time consuming. The four hundred square foot interior had a simple pull out bed, table, two chairs, and a full kitchen and bathroom space.

It was certainly far more comfortable accommodations than Mac had to endure on previous assignments and given the delicious smells coming from the multitude of Asian eateries on either side of the street, he was likely to be much better fed too.

Mac sat inside the apartment with the front door securely locked and waited for Tilley's scheduled call on his shadow cell. As usual for Ray Tilley, the call arrived on time.

"I take it you found the key to the apartment?"

Mac said yes, and then waited for Tilley to continue so he could find out where the ammo was being kept.

"Behind the fridge you'll find a safe. The combination is 09102001. You'll find a Truvelo 338 Counter Measure sniper rifle accompanied by forty rounds of ammunition. Are you familiar with the model?"

Mac had limited experience with Truvelo rifles but did recall they were both lightweight, and folded up for quick and easy storage making them useful when transporting from one location to another, though the lighter weight also diminished the weapon's accuracy if the target was beyond five hundred yards.

"A little, but I'm a quick study."

"Ok, you'll also find another file with Ramtin Armeen's known schedule, his address, a short list of people in Chicago who know him, etc. It's not terribly specific, but it's a start. He stays in a suite above his work office, so that should make things a little easier for you. The building is well secured though. As for Hamid Gilani we're not even sure he's in Chicago at this time. As soon as I confirm his location I'll let you know. Any questions?"

Mac moved from his chair to the small window that overlooked the crowded street below.

"Yeah, any preference on which one you'd like me to take out first? I assume Ramtin since he has the means to pay for passage out of the country and then hole up somewhere safe and that's exactly what he'd do if he found out Gilani was killed. As for Gilani, once Ramtin is dead he'll likely panic and reveal himself and I can track him down soon after."

There was a brief pause before Tilley replied.

"That sounds fine, Mac, though if either presents a kill shot I'd suggest you take it. And be careful."

A moment later found Mac pulling back the apartment's fridge and finding the safe. He quickly input the digital combination given him and opened the door. Inside sat the scoped sniper rifle and the promised forty rounds of ammunition, a pair of high powered military grade Steiner binoculars with night vision capability, the Gilani file, and a well worn wallet containing his alternate identifications that included an Illinois drivers license, a passport, and grocery store discount card put there to make the wallet's contents appear that much more authentic. Mac took out the binoculars and the wallet and then closed the safe and pushed the fridge back into place. He then took another look at the Tilley-provided drivers license, noting his name was Mackenzie Wallace. He stuck the wallet into the front inside pocket of his navy blue windbreaker jacket.

Well that should be easy enough to remember.

He was hungry.

Food first and then a bit of night recon.

Mac stepped out onto the second floor stoop, locked the door, and then moved quickly down the stairs and onto the sidewalk below. He scanned both sides of the street and decided on a restaurant a half block down to the right named, *Uncle Chan's.*

The restaurant's interior eating area was no more than twelve feet wide but at least twice that long. Booths lined the right side of the wall and several two-chair tables took up space on the left. The place was empty but for an older black couple seated in the booth nearest the entrance. Mac was greeted almost immediately by an attractive twenty-something Asian woman who looked at him with a wide, friendly smile. "Is it just you for late lunch or would you like the dinner menu?"

Mac smiled back and shrugged.

"Whatever you suggest, ma'am – I am hungry. I'll take the booth all the way in the back if that's ok."

The woman's eyes widened as did her smile.

"Ah, are you southern?"

Mac nodded as he followed the woman toward the back booth. If possible he always took a table near the back in a restaurant so as to be able to see anyone coming into the place. It was a lesson first taught to him many years earlier by his father during Mac's childhood growing up in Carville, Louisiana.

"Yes ma'am."

The young woman motioned for Mac to take a seat and then proceeded to pour him a glass of water into a red plastic cup.

"Do you live here in Chicago?"

Mac noted the woman's English was excellent, with just a hint of an Asian accent.

"No, I'm on business."

The woman nodded while the smile remained.

"Yes, always lots of business here. My name is Li. Do you want to look at both the lunch and dinner menus? We don't mind. It's late afternoon so…"

Mac smiled.

"Hello, Li, my name is Mac. How about you just bring me the dish that you think will best fill the belly of a sad sack like me. I don't mind spending a little extra."

Li nodded and then disappeared through a small hallway behind Mac's booth where he could hear the sound of kitchen activity.

Mac looked up at the sound of the front door opening and watched as a tall, early twenties black male dressed in a grey hoodie and a pair of dark jeans that hung well below his waist entered the restaurant. While appearing outwardly to ignore the new arrival Mac Walker was in fact assessing the man's threat potential, a habit of many years both in the military and as a member of Project Icon.

"Hey, where do you want me to sit?"

The older black couple eating toward the front of the restaurant looked up, annoyed by the volume of the younger man's voice. Unfortunately for them, this did not go unnoticed.

"You got a problem with me being here?"

The couple looked down at the table, hoping their silence would somehow make them invisible to the overtly aggressive new arrival. Mac heard motion behind him and then saw Li walking quickly toward the front of the restaurant.

"Hello, sir, you can sit in a booth here if you want. Can I get you anything to drink?"

Mac sensed the tension in Li's voice, though he was impressed by her composure as the man loomed above her.

"Yeah, bitch, get me a Coke."

Li looked like she was ready to ask the man to leave but then simply smiled and nodded as the man sat down in the booth directly behind the older couple.

Mac noted the man's right foot as it rapidly tapped the cream-colored tile restaurant floor. He appeared increasingly agitated, his eyes nervously glancing through the large windows overlooking the still busy street outside.

Don't do something stupid, hood-rat. Just drink your Coke and let me eat my own meal in peace.

Li returned from the kitchen and stopped at Mac's table first to pour him a cup of hot tea. Her hands were trembling slightly as she did so.

"You ok, Li?"

Her face contorted into a forced half smile while she nodded.

"I'm fine, just part of the job having to deal with assholes like him, right? Your food will be ready in just a few more minutes."

"Bitch, where's my Coke?"

Li rolled her eyes and then whispered to Mac.

"I'm sorry. We don't normally get people like him in here."

Mac placed his right hand gently on top of Li's and shrugged.

"No need to apologize. Like you said, it's just the unfortunate part of the job sometimes."

"Young man, do you really have to talk to people like that?"

Mac winced. It was the husband seated at the front of the restaurant. While Mac respected the older man's decision to say something, he knew it would likely escalate a situation he hoped would have soon faded out of on its own. Instead it would give the younger man the excuse to go full on dipshit.

And that means I have to get involved.

"What did you say, old man? Shut your tired ass. And tell your bitch to stop looking at me like that. Dried up old skank, get your ass out of here!"

The older man stood up. Mac guessed his age to be near seventy. He was nicely dressed in a dark brown sport coat and tan slacks, a reminder of a time when people rarely went out in public without looking respectable. It was a stark contrast to the younger black man's pathetic attempt at an apparently more modern fashion statement. If so, modern certainly didn't appear to be better.

"You don't talk to my wife like that. Now why don't you just leave?"

The man's voice was shaking slightly, betraying his fear in confronting the younger man who was already pushing himself up out of the booth.

Mac took a sip from his tea and then slowly set the small white cup back onto the table, knowing his own personal sense of duty and honor required he intervene.

Shit.

"You want to try and make me leave, old man?"

Li called out from behind the younger man.

"Sir, you need to get out of here or I am going to call the police."

"No, I don't think so, bitch. Get my goddamn Coke! I'm sick and tired of you slant-eyes not wanting to serve people like me! Racist little dog eatin' yellow skinned motherfu---"

"Time for you to move on, hood-rat."

The black man's eyes widened as he looked to be noticing Mac Walker for the first time.

"What? What did you just call me, white boy?"

Mac positioned himself between Li and the black man and was grateful to see the older couple scurrying out the door.

"I called you a hood-rat, because that's what you are. Not because of your skin color or even those jeans that are about ready to fall down around your ankles like some prison queen signaling to all the other inmates they should line up and take their turn. No, you're a hood-rat because that's your personality. A useless, ill-mannered piece of shit who comes into a place like this and bothers good people just trying to have a nice meal. You see, hood-rat, I got a date with a nice plate of something good, and I intend to keep that date without having to smell your stink. So you turn that candy-ass around and get the hell out of here before you rile something up in me that will mess your shit up eight ways to Sunday, son."

The younger man's eyes blinked several times as his mouth fell open. He had lived several years where his size and aggressive nature caused others around him to defer to his repeated intimidations with few challenges. Even the neighborhood cops did their best to avoid dealing with him.

Mac turned halfway around to glance at Li.

"Is there going to be wonton soup with my meal?"

Li appeared confused by the question, but nodded her head anyways. Mac turned back to face the man he called hood-rat, the former Navy SEAL looking even more serious and determined than before.

"Ok, that makes your situation even *more* precarious hood-rat. You see, I just *love* wonton soup. It's like Asian gumbo, you know? So if you keep standing here convinced you're actually some kind of legitimate bad-ass, or whatever it is you think you're doing, and you make my wonton go cold, *I just might have to kill you.*"

"Hood-Rat" looked at Mac as if the special ops veteran had suddenly grown a second head.

"What are you on about, man? Sit your raggedy old ass down!"

Mac watched as the younger man once again glanced nervously to the street outside.
He plans to rob the place.

"Hey, look at me. *Right here*, look me in the eyes."

Hood-rat puffed out his chest as he turned to face Mac Walker. The unfortunate Chicago native knew nothing of Mac's intense military training and experience, or the fact he had killed many and killed often in nearly every gone to hell corner of the globe. Instead he saw a white man of forty or so years of age who was of average height and build with closely cropped hair that was already going grey on the sides dressed in a simple blue jacket and jeans.

There was something in Mac's eyes though that made the younger man pause. It was an unusual mix of certain confidence, glowering intensity and total absence of fear.

"What's your name, son?"

Hood-rat's face tightened as he grunted at Mac and then pulled the front right side of his sweatshirt up to reveal a handgun stuffed into the low slung waist of his jeans.

Mac's initial reaction was a thin smile which unnerved hood-rat even more as once again he found himself confused over the older man's lack of even the faintest hint of fear.

"My name is shoot you dead if you don't back off."

With the thin smile remaining on his face, Mac slowly opened the front of his jacket to reveal his always present SIG P226 issued to him during his SEAL days, personally modified by him to improve upon its already quick fire capabilities.

"Hey, I got one of those too! Now you don't want to try and draw on *me*, hood-rat. This just isn't your day. I'm sorry, but the thing is, you are seriously out of your element here. Now I'm going to ask you reeeaaaaaal nice to just turn around and walk on out."

Hood-rat stood momentarily frozen, his gaze darting around the restaurant's small interior in an attempt to avoid looking into Mac's eyes.

While watching every twitch from the suddenly silent hood-rat, Mac's voice called out in soft, even tones to Li who remained standing behind him.

"Li, who's in the kitchen?"

Li's voice was not nearly so calm as Mac's. She was trying very hard to remain composed, but Mac sensed she could easily be pushed into outright panic.

"My mother and father, it's just them."

Mac nodded slowly, sensing hood-rat growing more panicked as well.

"Ok, I want you to go back there and wait just a bit. I'll have this trash taken out soon. There's no need to call the police. Oh, and keep the soup hot for me, ok?"

Mac waited for the sounds of Li's departure to indicate she was safely in the kitchen before he once again turned his full attention back onto the young black man who moments earlier thought the restaurant to be an easy robbery opportunity for him. Mac was hoping to avoid involving the authorities for an incident he believed he could easily handle himself. There was no sense in him risking his cover so early in the assignment.

"I asked your name, but you don't seem too keen on telling me, so that means I have to keep calling you hood-rat. Now here's how this is about to go down. You're ready to get real stupid, and that means you're stepping into *my* world. Now in this world, I protect good people who are working hard every day trying to make a living serving good food at reasonable prices. Now who doesn't like good food at reasonable prices? Assholes like you, that's who. The thing is you don't know a damn thing about hard work, do you? No, you'd rather just take what isn't yours. You think you're entitled to it because you have a gun and you think society has somehow done you wrong. Or maybe you're just another piece of shit bully who likes making people feel afraid and unsafe. Well, this time you picked the wrong place, the wrong time, and you sure as hell picked the wrong guy to mess with, hood-rat."

Mac's voice lowered to a whispered snarl as his eyes appeared lit by a righteous fire that would scorch any foolish enough to challenge him.

"Now go ahead you pathetic pile of maggot shit and try and pull that piece and see what it gets you."

Hood-rat's real name was Tyrell Watts, a twenty-three year old product of the government subsidized and perpetually hopeless Chicago Southside. He had been in and out of Juvenile Detention since the age of twelve. At nineteen he was sentenced to a year for aggravated assault but actually served just four months. He came out harder and more convinced of his invulnerability than ever. Two weeks after his twenty-first birthday Tyrell committed his first murder, the shooting death of a neighborhood rival. The local authorities paid it little attention, already overwhelmed by the city's rampant homicide rate inside neighborhoods that seemed intent on killing one another. Last month while sitting inside a packed nightclub, Tyrell was among several other men who had exchanged gunfire with a rival gang. The news reported two were killed, though Tyrell had no idea if one of his bullets was responsible. He just fired several rounds and ran. Not that he cared either way. Death was simply a part of his day-to-day life.

The same kind of death he now was ready to deliver to this far too bold white dude who had apparently watched one too many John Wayne movies.

Mac's focus was at a level beyond what 99.99% of human beings knew to be possible. Perhaps some professional athletes who had achieved a point of domination in their particular sport would understand, but even they didn't play in an environment that was literally a quick succession of life and death half moments where failure often proved the very last mistake one was allowed to make. Even among his fellow soldiers Mac excelled at seeing a hostile's intent before anyone else. It was a quality that made him among the most dangerous of soldiers – and the most valuable. It was the same quality largely responsible for Bill Tilley picking him to lead Project Icon. And sadly for Tyrell Watts it would soon prove to be the same quality that would, as Mac so recently communicated to the Chicago street thug, *mess his shit up eight ways to Sunday*.

Tyrell was allowed to make his move, after which Mac's well honed and all too deadly instincts were unleashed.

The younger man's right hand only made it halfway to the gun at his waist before Mac's left hand encircled Tyrell's right wrist while the open palm of Mac's right hand slammed violently upward into the bottom half of Tyrell's chin. The force of impact caused Tyrell to bite down onto his own tongue, nearly severing the front portion off with his own teeth.

As Tyrell fell back in a half-conscious daze Mac smoothly followed the motion of the younger man's retreating body as he reached down with his right hand to remove the handgun and then slide it behind him with a kick of his right foot. Tyrell recovered just enough to attempt a pair of wild, awkward roundhouse swings with both hands which Mac avoided by simply moving his head back a few inches as each fist passed in front of him.

Tyrell emitted a high-pitched shriek as Mac's right foot then found an all too vulnerable home in the form of his nut-sack.

As the black man fell to his knees Mac stepped behind him and in one lighting-fast motion clamped his forearms together just under Tyrell's jaw. It was a move he learned from another member of Project Icon, a former soldier named Benjamin "Benny" Williams who might very well had been the single most capable hand-to-hand fighter in the entire U.S. military.

Benny called the move *killing the light,* a modified version of the common choke hold named so for its ability to quickly render an opponent unconscious or, if one continued applying pressure to the primary carotid arteries of the victim's neck, kill them.

Mac tightened his hold and then pulled back with his shoulders and was almost immediately rewarded with the sensation of the other man's body going limp. Mac held on for a few seconds longer before he released the hold. He then stood up, not bothering to lessen the impact of Tyrell's face hitting the restaurant floor.

The span of time between Tyrell reaching for his gun and Mac standing over his unconscious body was no more than seven seconds. Mac reached down to quickly make sure Tyrell was still breathing. Having confirmed that, he called back to the kitchen area.

"Li, could you come out here please?"

Li emerged from the back of the restaurant and then stopped several feet from where Mac stood over Tyrell's motionless body. Her eyes went wide as her mouth fell open in shock. Mac began waving both his hands in front of him.

"No-no-no, he's ok. I just decided he needed a little nap time. I was wondering if you knew someone you trust who drives a cab you might get them to drive him out to one of the South Side streets and drop him off?"

Li remained unmoving, her dark eyes darting from the body to Mac. A middle-aged Asian woman emerged from behind her and began pointing to Mac while speaking a language Mac vaguely recognized as Mandarin. Whatever the older woman said it seemed to shake Li from her shock as she nodded and then took out a phone from the front left pocket of her black slacks.

"I have a cousin who drives a cab. I can call him."

Mac winked, trying to let Li know everything was going to be fine.

"Good, get him here as soon as possible. Our friend probably won't be out for more than twenty minutes or so."

It was just over five minutes later that Mac Walker dropped Tyrell into the trunk of an older yellow cab as the man behind the wheel waited happily for his promised payment. Mac withdrew three crisp one hundred dollar bills and gave them to Li's cab-driving cousin, a mid-thirties balding Asian man who acted as if transporting an unconscious man to another part of town was just another day on the job.

"A hundred for the cab fare, and another two hundred for the trouble, thank you."

As the cab drove away, Li's voice called to him from within the restaurant.

"Sir, Mac, your meal is ready!"

Mac looked to his left and right, and then scanned the other side of the street and found nothing or no-one that appeared to be out of the ordinary just as his stomach growled – loudly.

Soon he was devouring every bit of his wanton soup and shrimp fried rice and washing it down with cups of steaming hot tea. Li brought more soup, rice and tea, telling him it was her family's honor to be serving him. Only when Mac admitted to not being able to eat another bite did both Li's parents emerge from the kitchen. It was the first time Mac had seen the father. He was barely over five feet, the result of a badly bent back, and incredibly thin, but his eyes indicated a powerful pride in owning his own business with his wife and daughter.

The man bowed his head to Mac and then his wife did the same. The older woman said something to Li while keeping her eyes fixed upon Mac.

"If you will still be in Chicago on business, my parents invite you to be their guest tomorrow evening in our home upstairs. They wish to introduce you to my grandmother, my father's mother. She is the one who made our voyage to American possible. If you cannot accept the invitation, I will understand, though they may not. Where they come from, it is a very rare thing to refuse such a request."

Mac had no idea what tomorrow might bring, but was determined to do his best to accept the family's kind offer. Plus, he couldn't ignore the fact Li was very attractive, and if Mac Walker suffered from any potential weakness, it was his inability to refuse a chance to spend more time with a pretty lady.

"What time would they want me here, Li?"

Li glanced at her mother and then answered.

"After we close. I know it makes it rather late, but would 10:00 work for you? We are right upstairs from the restaurant. I could meet you outside and bring you in."

Mac sensed Li was just as anxious to spend more time with him as well.

"I tell you what, if you can round up just one more bowl of that wonton soup, we have ourselves a date."

Li smiled and then spoke to both her parents who in turn nodded and smiled at Mac as if he had just made them the happiest people in all of Chicago.

As Mac sat happily working through his third bowl of soup he began contemplating what he would be doing later tonight.

I need to scope out Ramtin Armeen's building. Set up a surveillance post, and possible firing locations based on applicable entrance and exit points.

Mac's spoon paused halfway between bowl and mouth as he heard his shadow cell going off. He dropped the spoon and took the call. It was Tilley. Mac looked around to make certain no one was close enough to over-hear the phone conversation.

"Gilani is in Chicago, Mac. I personally confirmed from an NSA source. I'm also getting pressure from higher ups to have this completed within forty-eight hours. Call me when it's done."

Mac sat up in his booth and shook his head while pressing the phone against his ear.

"What? Forty-eight hours? I can't promise delivery on that! Who's pressuring you on the timeline, Ray? Is it the senator?"

Tilley paused long enough that Mac thought he might have already ended the call, but then his voice came back, betraying just a hint of the strain he was obviously under.

"We got some serious higher ups on this one, Mac. Get it done and Project Icon will be sitting real good with people who can bring us a lot of business. Anything less---"

"Anything less and they'll go with someone else. I understand how this business works, Ray, though it pisses me off when these bastards who call the shots from some D.C. office likely couldn't find their own ass in the dark. Forty-eight hours seems like just enough time to screw something up real bad. I'll do my best, but I don't like having something like this dropped on me the day I arrive. I know you said they wanted it done as quickly as possible, but I'd think they would want it done *right* more than just wanting it done *fast*. I feel sorry for their wives."

Tilley chuckled, both amused by the joke, and glad to hear Mac still had his often unique sense of humor. That meant his operative was not feeling entirely overwhelmed by the suddenly shortened operation schedule.

"I know, Mac, I know. Good luck."

Mac returned the shadow cell to the inside pocket of his jacket and then refocused on finishing his still warm soup, knowing that later tonight he would be sitting outside on the top of a building looking through a pair of night vision goggles while most likely freezing his ass off.

3.

"In three days Allah will know us to be among the greatest warriors of his will, Ramtin. Three days until the streets of America run red with the blood of its cursed spawn."

Ramtin Armeen sat behind the large custom glass desk inside the confines of his top floor private study overlooking Chicago's central business district. He regarded Hamid Gilani with a mix of gratitude and humor. The gratitude was for Hamid's unwavering dedication to the cause, and humor over the man's persistent religious fervor. Ramtin cared little about the fables of god and prophets. For him religion was nothing more than a convenient motivator to ensure action by those radicalized by their own hatred and insecurities.

"You've confirmed every location from the list?"

Hamid nodded.

"We have people prepared for every single one you gave us. Thirty-three locations: nine university campuses, seventeen public schools, and seven large daycare centers including the one here in Chicago. This is going to happen, Ramtin, praise Allah."

Ramtin folded his perfectly manicured fingers under his smooth-shaven chin and smiled.

"You've done very well, Hamid. I want you to know how grateful I am for your service to me."

Hamid gave Ramtin a short bow and then turned to leave before being stopped by the sound of Ramtin's voice.

"The American authorities are likely watching us, you know."

Hamid turned back around, communicating his indifference with a shrug of his shoulders.

"Let them watch. They have no idea of our plans though I will of course remain vigilant. And even if they suspect something, at this point they are out of time to stop us, and once completed, no evidence will exist that might implicate you, Allah willing of course."

Ramtin, resplendent in a custom tailored dark grey pinstriped business suit stood up from behind his desk and raised his arms to either side of him while looking back at Hamid with a satisfied gleam in his eyes.

"Allah willing, my friend, Allah willing…"

Hamid bowed again and then left Ramtin alone in the study.

The Iranian-born billionaire turned to stare out the window of his high-rise apartment overlooking the seemingly happy twinkling lights of nighttime Chicago. Though his outward appearance suggested a man entirely relaxed in the opulent and comforting surroundings of his home, Ramtin Armeen was actually barely able to contain his excitement over what was so soon to be the culmination of many months of careful planning and hoped for execution.

He knew America's reaction would prove as predictable as its inaction. They would demand more safety, and the kind of bigger government required to make that happen, just as they did after September 11th, 2001. And the larger and more costlier their own government became, the weaker they actually were, the more willing they would disarm, retreat, and ultimately, give up.

The United States was all too ready for its own self-inflicted defeat.

…Mac Walker could hardly believe his good luck in having his primary target looking out a window. There he was, Ramtin Armeen in all his arrogant and dangerous glory no more than three hundreds yards from Mac's own outdoor rooftop location.

The excellent military-grade Steiner binoculars allowed Mac to not only see Armeen, but make out some of the details of his study as well. The Project Icon operative then scanned the outline of the window, trying to confirm something he already suspected.

Ah, there it is.

The "it" was an Amidan company logo in the upper right frame of the window. Mac knew Amidan specialized in bullet resistant glass. Attempting to snipe Ramtin from a rooftop location from three hundred yards was not going to be an option. What was required then was an up-close approach, which meant Mac was likely going to have to find access into and then out of Ramtin's apartment building.

Mac scanned the building entrance and quickly located a tall, heavily built doorman who was most likely armed. Just inside the door was a black-suited, middle-aged man providing yet more security. A surveillance camera was located just above the entrance door to record everyone entering and leaving the building. Mac knew that trying to enter via the front door without an invitation was unlikely, at least not without creating a confrontation between him and the building's security staff which in turn would alert Ramtin to his presence.

Have to find a way to sneak in…

Mac's eyes suddenly narrowed behind the lenses of the Steiner binoculars as he panned back to the apartment building rooftop.

He was certain he had seen a blur of movement as something moved quickly behind a large metallic heating duct. Mac remained looking at the rooftop for several more minutes in an attempt to confirm someone was in fact there, but he saw nothing.

A bird or trick of the light?

Even as he made the thought, Mac knew better. Someone had been on that roof. The questions left to him were *who* and *why*.

…Hamid smiled in the darkness, a mere shadow of a shadow as he continued to stare across the night chasm separating him from the other man who stood on another rooftop across the street. Whoever the man was, Hamid knew he had been looking into Ramtin's window, confirming what they already suspected – they were in fact being watched.

Who might you be? FBI? CIA? Perhaps Homeland Security? Ah, it doesn't matter, I will kill you regardless. Perhaps feed you to the pigs as I did the last one they sent.

As Mac Walker made his way from the rooftop back to the street, so too did Hamid Gilani, the confident smile still affixed to the jihadi militant's smoothly shaved face.

By the time Mac was in his rental car returning to the Chinatown safe house, Hamid was following two cars back in a late model black Range Rover. Mac glanced several times into his rearview mirror to make certain he wasn't being followed while making several random turns onto side streets. Soon he confirmed the Range Rover remained behind him.

The rented four door sedan shot forward as Mac pushed down on the accelerator. He glanced back once again to see how the unknown to him driver of the Range Rover would respond.

"Dammit."

Mac spoke the words as his rearview mirror filled up with the flashing lights of a Chicago police cruiser. The Range Rover had disappeared.

Maybe I wasn't being followed.

Soon a middle-aged African American Chicago cop was standing alongside Mac's vehicle asking for his license. Mac gave the officer his assignment-created identification and then waited patiently behind the wheel, curious to see if the manufactured identification Tilley had given him would prove acceptable to a basic law enforcement check.

"You know why I stopped you, sir?"

Mac nodded.

"Yeah, I was speeding, changed lanes several times without signaling, probably swerved pretty good once or twice back there as well. Take your pick. The good news though, at least this time is I haven't been drinking - yet."

The mustached police officer scowled down at Mac.

"You trying to be a smart-ass, sir?"

It was then Mac remembered his sidearm holstered inside his jacket. Chicago was a city with quite possibly the most prohibitive gun laws in the country, and if the officer decided to have him step out of the car and frisk him, the situation could turn into something far more serious.

I sure as hell can't get allow myself to be thrown into a holding cell.

"No, officer, I was just being honest. I'm here on business and don't know the streets too well."

The officer stared at Mac intensely for several seconds and then glanced to the rental car's back seat. Mac knew the officer was trying to determine if he was under the influence of alcohol or drugs.

"What kind of business are you doing at this hour of the night, sir?"

Mac scrambled to come up with a plausible example that he hoped would alleviate further suspicion.

"Well, I guess you could call it the kind of business I wouldn't want my girlfriend to know about."

The police officer's bemused expression indicated he understood the implications of Mac's answer.

"I'll be right back, sir. Just sit tight."

Mac knew his assignment identification was about to be tested.

The officer returned soon after and handed Mac his driver's license.

"I am going to let you off with a warning, Mr. Wallace. I think it best you get back to wherever you need to go, but do it a little slower and a lot less erratically, ok?"

Mac looked up and nodded, trying to appear as grateful as possible.

"Thank you, officer. I'll sure do that."

Soon Mac made his way back to the Chinatown safe-house location, where he parked his vehicle in the alleyway adjacent to the apartment's entrance steps. A heavy layer of low clouds blocked out any moonlight, making the alley that much darker. As Mac locked the car he glanced behind him, feeling as if he was being watched. His right hand instinctively withdrew his sidearm from its holster. The other end of the alley, what little he could see of it, appeared empty. He then walked out onto the street and glanced to his left and right, making certain there was no sign of the Range Rover he thought to be following him earlier.

Mac grunted to himself as he turned to make his way quickly up the apartment stairs.

Get a grip, Mac. You're acting like some kid who's afraid of the dark.

As Mac closed and locked the heavy-framed safe-house door, Ramtin Armeen stepped out from the alleyway darkness that had hidden him so well.

It appeared the pigs would soon be enjoying another meal.

4.

Tilley sounded like he was about ready to lose his shit, and that made Mac that much more nervous for what could be coming.

"Some of us think the list of schools overheard during our surveillance was misdirection, or that they've picked new targets since going silent. Fact is, Mac we're flying blind here. All we have are Armeen and Gilani there in Chicago. We need them gone. If we just bring them in, the operation will likely continue as planned. Hell, if anything, we give them both an alibi. We'd have them in custody and the terror cells would proceed as planned. Then their lawyers would kick our ass."

"I'm doing my best on this end, Ray. Give me another twenty-four hours and I should have this thing taken care of. I'll let you know more tonight."

Mac ended the call and put his jacket on, then double-checked to make certain his weapon was properly secured in its shoulder holster.

It was going to be one hell of a busy day.

The early morning Chicago air helped to wake him up which was good, because he had slept just a few hours on the uncomfortable studio apartment's pull out bed, finally waking both groggy and sore.

Need a good strong cup of coffee to start this day off right.

Mac bounded down the narrow apartment steps and made his way to his parked car. Already the city was alive with the sounds of a new day as a multitude of vehicles drove past the alley's entrance.

Overhead the clouds parted, allowing the alleyway to be momentarily filled with sunlight.

Someone's behind me!

Mac began to turn so he could face the source of the soft shuffling noise as his right hand reached into his jacket to withdraw his weapon. If he had reacted a half second sooner, he might have succeeded in defending himself.

That half-second hesitation cost him dearly.

A half-inch thick iron rod smashed into the left side of Mac's skull sending him crashing into the side of the rental car. Even though his vision went momentarily dark, Mac instinctively pushed himself away from the vehicle with his hands up in front of his head trying desperately to avoid being hit in the head again, knowing he might not survive a another blow as brutal as the first.

The second strike arrived with a dull clanging thud against the top of Mac's right kneecap. Mac couldn't stop himself from falling forward onto the pavement below as he willed his vision to clear enough to allow him to see his assailant.

It was Hamid Gilani's confident and smiling face that loomed over the former Navy SEAL.

"I don't know who you are, but I will soon enough."

Mac saw death in Gilani's eyes, and the thought of being taken out by scum such as him infuriated the military operative. His right hand found the inside of his jacket and closed around the space where his sidearm was located.

Unfortunately, Mac's weapon was no longer there. He looked up to see Hamid Gilani holding it in his left hand as he shook his head at Mac.

"Is this what you were looking for?"

Gilani's right hand rose up over his head and then sent the end of the iron pipe into the side of Mac's left jaw, causing his vision to detonate into varying shades of brilliant white before suddenly going dark.

Don't lose consciousness...

Gilani used the heavy pipe to strike down upon Mac's head, neck, shoulders and chest, each blow pushing Mac closer and closer toward oblivion until finally even his seemingly unending resilience and determination gave way to darkness.

Two hours later.

"You see, I told you he was still alive! This one is much stronger than the CIA bitch you brought here."

Mac's eyes felt too heavy to open, but he could hear the conversation taking place around him. There was also the terrible smell, and the constant squealing of pigs.

Lots and lots of pigs.

Mac took several deep measured breaths in an attempt to push back the debilitating pain that covered the entirety of his body.

"Look at me."

Mac tried to pull his head upward toward the voice but found the effort too great.

"I said look at me."

The voice was deep, calm, almost soothing. It was the same voice Mac had head in the alley just before the attack.

Gilani.

The name reverberated inside Mac's skull. He slowly opened his mouth and then closed it, trying to determine if his jaw was broken.

"Who sent you?"

Mac's eyes partially opened though his vision provided nothing more than a cloudy mix of off-white colors and darker shadows. Mac realized then he was suffering from the symptoms of a likely concussion.

"Good, now tell me who sent you?"

Mac cleared his throat and willed his vision to clear until finally, Hamid Gilani's face came more fully into focus directly in front of him.

"Do you know who I am?"

Mac nodded and then smiled as his eyes closed while he mumbled a reply.

"Pig farmer."

Gilani cursed in Arabic as the sound of laughter erupted from behind him.

"His brains are scrambled. He doesn't know what has happened to him!"

Mac didn't recognize the second voice but assumed it was the owner of the pigs responsible for the smell that remained a noxious blanket over whatever God forsaken place he had managed to get himself dumped into. Gilani's angry retort cut through the other man's laughter.

"I don't have time for jokes, Allid! Are your pigs ready?"

Allid Safarah was a forty-nine year old Lebanese immigrant who had come to the United States nearly ten years ago after learning his only uncle had left him a forty-acre pig farm some thirty miles north of Chicago. As a devout Muslim, Allid refused to eat pork, but he delighted in raising them, overseeing their breeding, butchering, and sale of the meat, though he had come to derive his greatest pleasure from their feeding. The pigs amazed Allid with their ability to devour almost anything left in their pen, especially if he starved them for a day or two. He had once watched them make an entire truck tire disappear.

It was five years earlier when, after having not fed them for three days, Allid watched as several of the strongest pigs suddenly turned on an older, arthritic sow who had been struggling to walk for months. Within the cacophony of shrieking hogs, Allid was mesmerized as he watched the other pigs tear into the sow, pushing her down into the mud and ripping her apart, their jaws covered in blood and muck as they happily gorged themselves on one of their own.

Soon Allid was throwing an assortment of other crippled animals into the pig pen and watching them be devoured as if the wretched creatures had never been there at all. The hogs' appetite for flesh grew with every tasty morsel Allid brought to them.

He began dreaming of feeding the animals a live human being, so much so the idea pushed aside all other obligations. Allid found himself fantasizing to images of someone screaming as the pigs descended upon them, those cries soon turning to the wet smacking sounds of happy pigs enjoying another treat.

Fortune smiled upon him when a chance encounter at the largest Muslim mosque in Chicago brought Allid Safarah and Hamid Gilani together. Gilani had a very specific problem, one which Allid promised he could provide an equally specific solution to.

The CIA agent was near death when Allid dumped her body into the pen, but soon enough panicked realization of what was about to happen awakened her senses. She unleashed a wonderful chorus of terrified screams as the first few pigs tore into her and were then quickly joined by the rest of the drove.

It took no more than a half day for every bit of the CIA agent to disappear. Even her shoes and clothing were greedily devoured.

And now here is another American for my pigs! Allah continues to bless me!

"They were fed late yesterday so may not be as hungry as they were the last time you were here, Hamid. You gave me no indication you would be arriving this morning so I've had no time to prepare them."

Gilani was about to comment when his cell phone rang. He turned and walked several feet away from Allid to ensure the conversation could not be overheard.

"Hamid, where are you?"

Gilani glanced toward Allid and then turned away, keeping his voice to a whisper.

"At the farm, why?"

Ramtin was nearly shouting.

"Why? We have a situation here! The entire plan is at stake! Have you killed the suspected spy yet?"

"No, I just started to interrogate him."

Gilani moved the phone away from his ear several inches as Ramtin unleashed a barrage of profanities.

"Kill him and be done with it! One of our Atlanta operatives has been detained by the authorities. I need you back here now!"

Gilani looked up to see Allid staring back at him as the pigs began to fight loudly among themselves.

"Ok, I will be there within the hour."

Allid's round fleshy face broke out into a wide, beaming smile. Gilani noted how the pig farmer had taken on an appearance very similar to that of the hogs he loved so much.

"They sense I have another meal for them! They grow restless."

Gilani made his way back to Mac who had remained sitting in the mud, his back resting against the thick wire meshed fence that made up one of several pens the animals were rotated into and out of throughout the large property. Mac's pen was separated from one filled with a mass of pigs by a single wood and wire mesh gate.

"This gun of yours is military issue isn't it?"

Mac knew the more he kept Gilani talking, the more time he would have to rebuild his own strength.

"Yeah, I was a SEAL."

Gilani nodded in mock admiration.

"Ah, a tough guy, eh? Hmmm…you don't look so tough. And what are you now, some kind of soldier for hire?"

Mac opened his eyes fully, ignoring how it worsened an already excruciating headache.

"Yeah, something like that."

Gilani's wide smile remained as he suddenly pressed Mac's own weapon against his forehead while also holding Mac's identification.

"It says here your name is Mackenzie Wallace. That isn't your real name though, is it?"

Mac's eyes closed and his chin dropped down against his chest, giving him the appearance of almost passing out again. He mumbled a reply.

"No."

Gilani pressed the gun against Mac's head with greater force.

"What's your real name?"

Mac sat silent and unmoving. Galini took his left hand and slapped him across the face.

"Hey! I asked you your name!"

Mac's eyes opened half way.

"Walker…Mac Walker."

"Good, now we can talk honestly! So, *Mac Walker*, why were you on that rooftop last night?"

Mac cleared his throat and then tried to spit but succeeded in only producing a thick line of drool that hung off his lower lip.

"I was doing surveillance."

Gilani leaned down more closely to Mac's face and whispered his next question.

"Who were you watching? Be truthful and I promise you a quick and relatively painless death."

Mac winced as another blinding shot of pain arced across his skull.

"Some guy named Armeen. I don't know who he is. I was just hired by an overseas client to confirm he was in Chicago. That's all I know. They gave me a photograph and I confirmed he was in the building. I called the client back and told him Armeen was in fact in Chicago. The job was done and then you got the drop on me and now I'm sitting here ass-deep in pig shit."

Mac hid his own satisfaction as he saw doubt flash across Gilani's eyes.

Go ahead, ask who hired me you terrorist prick.

"Who was the client, Mr. Walker? Who were you working for?"

Mac pushed his shoulders back against the pen's mesh fence.

"I don't know their name. They said they represented the Iranian government and were investigating a possible financial scandal. That's all they told me. It was just a simple job – confirm the guy was in Chicago. I don't know anything more than that."

Gilani appeared to be almost convinced Mac actually had nothing to do with trying to stop the next day's planned terror cell attacks.

"Will you be contacting them again?"

Mac slowly moved his head with a weak nod, his voice sounding as if the formation of each word required absolute focus.

"Yeah, this afternoon I'm supposed to check in with them one last time."

Gilani's face was an increasingly confused map of uncertainty. He wanted to simply kill Mac and be done with it, but worried about possible repercussions if Mac's Iranian information proved true. Ramtin feared few things in this world, but Gilani knew the billionaire to be increasingly wary of the Iranian government and its potential authority over a large portion of his company assets, assets essential to Gilani's own goal of bringing never-ending and bloody jihad to the western world.

Gilani handed Mac's SIG P226 to Allid.

"If he tries to get up, shoot him. I must return to Chicago but will be back this afternoon."

Allid looked at Mac and then glanced over to the awaiting horde of increasingly agitated pigs in the pen adjacent to the one Mac sat in. The Lebanese pig farmer's brow furrowed as he shared his discontent over the idea of killing Mac outright, his voice taking on a tone of a whining child.

"I want him alive when he's fed to the pigs. It makes it more…interesting."

Gilani didn't bother to hide his disgust and contempt for the pig farmer.

"Fine, whatever, he is not to leave that pen though, understood? I may be returning with Mr. Armeen. This American may have information useful to him."

Allid's eyes grew wide.

"Ramtin Armeen is coming here, *today*?"

Gilani was already walking to his black Range Rover. He wanted very badly to be away from the stink of the pigs and the equally repulsive Allid.

"Perhaps, but regardless, the American is to remain in that pen until I contact you later, though if he attempts to escape, you are to kill him."

Allid's fleshy face looked down at Mac, his beady eyes shining with excitement over the prospect of another human feeding.

Mac Walker didn't care about Allid's plans for him. Every minute the former soldier remained alive was a minute stronger both his mind and body became. Mac had fabricated his working for the Iranians of course. The ruse had succeeded in buying him needed time. It was a proverbial bullet in the dark which Mac was very happy to realize had most likely just saved him from an all too literal bullet to his own head.

What the smugly smiling pig farmer didn't realize is that Mac had been steadily loosening the rope that bound his hands and using the mud that covered the ground beneath him to lubricate his wrists and further wet the rope, making it expand further. As Gilani's vehicle disappeared on its journey back to Chicago, Mac Walker sat staring back at Allid with hands that were by then nearly free.

Adding to Allid's unknown-to-him and increasingly precarious situation was the fact he was holding a weapon Mac Walker had personally customized for his own use. The SIG P226 came manufactured with already reasonable semi-automatic quick firing capabilities, but Mac had modified it to a fully automated weapon with a far lighter trigger-pull than its factory specs. That alteration required he also improve the sidearm's safety features as well, an alteration Allid Safarah had no idea how to operate, thus rendering the gun in the Muslim pig farmer's hands into little more than an intimidating looking paperweight.

"The last one of you I fed to my pigs screamed *very* loudly. You think you are tough, but you will scream too. Oh yes, you will scream and scream and scream. And the more you scream, the hungrier they become."

The pounding inside Mac's head was finally lessening. His body ached, his vision not yet fully recovered, but he was alive. Allid was fatally oblivious to how much danger a still living, breathing, Mac Walker posed to him.

He would know soon enough...

5.

Ray Tilley had seen his share of interrogation footage over the years, but this particular example left him increasingly unsettled given the multiple coordinated attacks he felt to be imminent. The suspected Atlanta terror cell operative remained far too calm, confident, and evasive throughout the three hour long process.

His name was Yusuf Erdogen, a twenty-five year old Turkish citizen staying in the United States on a student visa. Federal authorities videotaped Erdogen picking up four high powered assault rifles from a representative of a known illegal arms dealer based out of Miami. Yusuf was directly linked to three other Middle Eastern students attending the same college - three students who then disappeared after Erdogen was detained by the FBI.

The FBI operatives grilled Yusuf repeatedly on the location of the missing students but were given nothing by Erdogen to assist in their location, and to make matters worse, Yusuf was demanding he be released to the Turkish consulate in Atlanta, a demand that had Senator Jackson Elder, seated directly across from Tilley, red-faced and cursing under his breath.

"The little son-of-a-bitch is demanding protection from the Turkish government! He named the consulate director, had the phone number for their Atlanta office...the kid knows exactly how to play our own system against us!"

Ray Tilley shared the senator's concerns. Clearly Yusuf Erdogen was far more than merely a student caught up in some conspiracy beyond his understanding. No, Erdogen was a willing participant in something that could prove as deadly and disruptive as the attacks of September 11th, 2001.

"What is Walker doing for us on this?"

Tilley shook his head.

"He's doing his best, Senator."

Senator Elder was not pleased by the response.

"His best? What the hell does that even mean? This thing is about to go off, Mr. Tilley. That boy in Atlanta is just a small part of what you and I both know is a much bigger operation."

Tilley's eyes returned to the screen showing the interrogation footage and then his office phone began ringing. The number indicated it was from his Atlanta contact.

This isn't gonna be good.

Senator Elder sat silently as he watched and listened to Tilley's brief phone conversation. By the time Tilley hung up, the senator already knew bad had gone to worse. Ray took a deep breath and then shared the new information.

"The FBI office in Atlanta just received a request from the Turkish consulate office there – from the consulate director himself."

The senator's mouth curled downward into a pronounced frown as he rolled his eyes.

"So what did they want? They expect us to give that kid over to them?"

Ray Tilley's own disbelief came out in the form of a soft grunt.

"Pretty much, that's exactly what they're demanding. Apparently Yusuf Erdogen is a nephew by marriage to the Corum Province governor who in turn is friendly with the Turkish Prime Minister."

The senator's face quickly progressed to a deepening shade or enraged purple.

"I don't give a shit if he's the goddamn King of Siam! That kid right there on the screen is involved in a planned terrorist attack against this country! We need to hold his ass in a cell until he gives us the information we need to eliminate the impending threat!"

Tilley agreed, but also knew such a seemingly logical expectation was beyond his, or even the senator's influence.

"I was told the FBI is handing the kid over to the Turkish consulate pending further investigation. Consulate officials are promising to cooperate fully with the investigation, though they did not agree to have Yusuf Erdogen remain in the United States during that time."

Senator Elder covered his face with both his hands as his shoulders slumped. His voice betrayed the politician's deepening fatigue and sense of betrayal.

"They're doing it again, Mr. Tilley. Just like with the 9/11 attacks…all those students with links to the Saudi Royal Family were flown out of the United States. Any potential leads, information…*gone*. This is the same damn thing!"

Tilley knew the senator spoke the truth. Whether intentional or not, the American government was aiding potential terrorists in covering their own tracks, and by doing so, putting innocent lives at risk.

"We still have Mac Walker, Senator. We still have a chance to cut off the head of this snake before it bites."

Ray Tilley withdrew his shadow cell and called Mac's number. He felt his stomach progressively tighten with each successive ring that left that call unanswered.

C'mon Mac, pick up your damn phone...

Mac heard his shadow cell ringing inside the right side pocket of Allid Safarah's jacket. The pig farmer withdrew the phone and glanced at it before looking up and smiling at his prisoner and then tossing the phone into the adjacent pen full of pigs. One of the larger sows grabbed it inside of her jaws and began crunching the device into oblivion.

"See, they eat *anything*, and soon they will be doing the same to you!"

Mac's face remained expressionless. He cared little about Allid's childish attempts to mock him. Instead, Mac continued to carefully pull and twist against the rope that bound his wrists behind him. It had been nearly an hour since Gilani's departure. Mac believed he had no more than another thirty minutes before Gilani and possibly others returned to the farm.

And when they do, I intend to be ready.

"You know America deserves what is coming, don't you?"

Mac ignored Allid's question.

"What we do is justice. The Muslim world has every right to revenge for the crimes the United States has inflicted upon it. Don't think for a moment you can sit upon your moral high horse and think yourself beyond our justice."

Mac shifted himself in the mud, pretending he wanted to face Allid directly when in fact he was using that movement to work more forcefully against his bonds.

"Did you say *high horse*? I thought you people ate horses?"

The fleshy skin of the pig farmer's face quivered as he shook his head angrily.

"What? No, we do not eat horses!"

Mac chuckled at how easy it was to confuse the over-confident and hapless Allid.

"Oh, my apologies, I must have been thinking of pigs. You love eating pigs, right?"

The Muslim pig farmer appeared horrified at the suggestion, pointing Mac's own weapon at him to emphasize his disapproval.

"Never! Such a thing is forbidden!"

"C'mon, man, don't you ever just want to bite into a big beautiful piece of bacon? Maybe a slice of ham with a couple eggs on the side?"

Allid eyes grew wider as his face contorted into an outraged snarl.

"You mock me? So close to death and yet you would say such things? "

Mac's hands were finally free, though he kept them hidden behind his back.

Allid lifted the Sig P226 above his head and attempted to shoot it into the air, not knowing the safety remained secured. Mac knew that meant he had to get moving before the pig farmer had time to react.

"This gun…how do you shoot it?"

Mac was pushing himself halfway back up onto his feet when he heard Allid's question.

This idiot is actually asking for instruction on how to use my own weapon against me?

The back of both Mac's legs were gripped by terrible cramping as the muscles screamed in protest over being forced to once again support his full weight. Mac ignored the pain and grasped the top of the pen fence to pull himself over, much to the shock of Allid who was falling backward waving the safety-locked gun in front of him.

"Get back! Back!"

The pig farmer continued to cry for Mac to get back into the pen. By then Mac was convinced Allid Safarah possessed an intellect rivaled only by a very dull and rusted collection of rarely used garden tools.

With the muscles of his legs already warming to the task, it took Mac no more than a few seconds to reach the pig farmer, grab his right wrist, and rip the weapon from his hands.

"I think this is mine, asshole."

It was Mac Walker who then pointed a gun at Allid, though this time the weapon's safety was no longer engaged.

"Please, I don't know anything! They just use my pigs to...you know."

Mac was in no mood for understanding, recalling the pig farmer's recent boast of how he disposed of the female CIA agent and how the same would be done to Mac. The Muslim was more of an animal than the assortment of hogs he kept.

"Yeah, I know – now get your fat ass in there with the pigs."

Allid shook his head frantically from side to side.

"No-no-no, that is not possible! You might as well shoot me right now."

Mac shrugged.

"Ok."

A single shot ripped a hole through the black rubber at the top of Allid's right boot. The pig farmer instantly fell to the muddy ground below screaming as both his hands grabbed onto his punctured foot. Mac then pointed his weapon at the pig farmer's face.

"You want me to shoot you again?"

Allid shook his head as his eyes avoided looking at Mac.

"Fine, then get in the pen."

Allid hobbled to the pen's small gate and opened it while he also issued a loud hissing noise that caused the pigs to back several feet away from him, though a few snorted loudly while several more let out an assortment of high pitched squeals.

"I think they might smell the blood filling up that boot of yours. Tell you what, Allid, you start talking and I won't shoot you in the other foot."

The pig farmer's eyes rolled erratically inside his oversized skull as he waved his hands rapidly in front of himself.

"I told you, I don't know anything!"

Mac saw Allid's eyes glance at the dilapidated farmhouse that sat a hundred yards north of the pig pens.

"How much they pay you for the use of your pigs, Allid?"

The pig farmer looked down at the ground hoping to again hide his eyes from Mac's gaze.

"That is not your business. I want to speak to a lawyer."

The comment genuinely stunned Mac. So much so he momentarily lowered his weapon.

"What?"

Allid straightened his shoulders and puffed his chest out, thinking he had discovered a way to threaten Mac Walker.

"You heard me. I want to speak to a lawyer! I have rights and *you* are in very big trouble!"

"Allid, I'm sorry to disappoint you, but you have no rights here. I'm not a cop so you can forget about speaking to some lawyer."

The pig farmer's facial expressions became even more exaggerated as he looked upward into the sky above him.

"Who are you? Why do you do this? I did not bring you here. It was not my choice. Please, don't hurt me."

Mac silently noted how Allid had gone from pathetically stupid to just pathetic. It all seemed….

He's stalling, hoping Gilani is on his way back.

Perhaps Allid was not as hopelessly ignorant as his behavior suggested. He may not have been smart, but it would seem he was more than capable of attempting to be clever. Mac once again pointed his weapon at Allid's head.

"Your time is up, Allid. If you have nothing to tell me, I have no reason to keep you alive."

For a half moment Allid was certain the American was bluffing, but then he looked into Mac Walker's eyes and saw the truth of the threat placed against him.

"Perhaps I know something of a plan."

Mac lowered his gun halfway as his eyes narrowed.

"No games, just tell me what you know."

The right corner of the pig farmer's mouth quivered as he suppressed a smile. He was certain he had just bought himself more time.

"I know they are preparing to do something – something *big*, something soon."

Mac shook his head.

"You're talking but you're not saying anything, Allid. I warned you, no games."

Another shot rang out as a bullet tore the lower half of Allid's left ear off.

"You shot me in the head! I'm bleeding! I'm bleeding!"

Mac's mouth was a grim slash across a face covered in two day's worth of stubble. He growled a warning while keeping his weapon pointed at Allid's head.

"Last chance, Allid…tell me what you know."

The pigs grew increasingly restless, their hungry squeals sounding more urgent as they inhaled the smell of Allid's fresh wound that dripped blood from the remnants of his ear lobe onto the muddy ground.

"You said you wouldn't shoot me again! You lied!"

"No, what I said was I wouldn't shoot you in the foot again. And that was a promise made only if you started giving me information – *real* information. Your pigs sound hungry."

The hogs gathered no more than six feet from Allid, their beady dark eyes regarding their caretaker with a new urgency born of a taste for flesh he had so enthusiastically instilled in them.

"Take off your jacket."

Allid looked at Mac as if the American had gone insane.

"Why?"

"Because I said – now take it off and hand it to me."

Allid did as he was told, his hands noticeably shaking as Mac took the jacket from him.

"Get on your knees."

The color faded from Allid's face as he realized he was going to die. The American was a far more capable adversary than Hamid had apparently thought him to be.

Hamid's arrogance is my own death! Why would Allah allow such a thing?

The pig farmer looked up and realized Mac's earlier deception.

"You aren't working for the Iranian government."

Mac grunted as he shook his head slowly. The pigs pushed within a few feet of Allid though they had grown strangely quiet.

"That CIA agent who was brought here, was she really alive when you fed her to those pigs?"

Allid sneered back up at Mac, suddenly finding a brief moment of courage.

"Yes! I told you already, the bitch screamed, and screamed loudly."

Mac Walker watched the hogs as they edged closer to Allid's injured foot and then looked into the pig farmer's eyes one last time.

"Ok, I guess this is one of those *what comes around goes around* moments."

As Mac turned around to make his way toward the house, Allid shouted from behind him as the pigs suddenly unleashed a barrage of intensely aggressive squeals.

"Allah will protect me! Allah will---"

The pig farmer began to scream.

Loudly.

6.

The interior of Allid's farmhouse somehow managed to be even more dilapidated than the outside, and the stink was worse as well, a mix of rotted wood, pest droppings, and old food. Mac quickly looked through the main areas of the low-ceilinged kitchen and living room but found nothing beyond piles of garbage strewn about the space.

Upstairs proved no better. Allid's room was at the end of the hallway and contained a single bed and unwashed clothes left scattered over the floor. Two other rooms were nearly empty as was the small hallway bathroom.

The cellar.

Mac made his way back downstairs and located the cellar door inside a small room adjacent to the kitchen that had at one time been a pantry but now contained bags of garbage piled ceiling high to the right and left of a narrow and locked doorway. The dirt covered linoleum was well worn leading to the cellar door, indicating Allid had made his way into and out of the cellar often. Mac unholstered his sidearm and proceeded to shoot the lock off and then kicked the door open.

The cellar gloom was disrupted by a single overhead light bulb hanging from the ceiling at the bottom of a set of rickety stairs in serious need of repair. Several of the steps were broken and the railing leaned inward as the wood connecting it to the stair frame was falling apart, destroyed by moisture and decades of neglect.

Mac moved carefully down the steps with his weapon drawn. He paused as he heard the sound of faint humming coming to his left. The light bulb above flickered with each step he took toward the dirt covered cellar floor.

The entire cellar was no more than a thirty by thirty space, with the home's plumbing lines running a foot above Mac's head and a myriad of electrical chords carrying power to other locations throughout the home. Mac glanced left and saw the source of the humming. It was a small desk and computer and a single, well worn lime green painted wooden chair.

After glancing once more around the cellar to ensure he was in fact alone, Mac moved toward the pig farmer's makeshift workspace. He touched the mouse and was rewarded with the screen illuminating.

Guess he couldn't be bothered to try and remember a pass-code.

A quick check of the computer's history showed nothing more than an affinity for pornography, weather reports, and online gambling. Allid appeared to have no email account. Mac was about to turn away from the desk when he noticed an icon in the upper left corner of the computer screen. It was a green and white Islamic star and crescent.

Mac clicked on the icon and was greeted by the outdated computer emitting a series of electronic wheezing noises as it struggled to load whatever data it was retrieving. After several stop and start seconds, the computer pulled up a series of images that left even a man as battle-hardened as Mac Walker, sickened.

The photos showed an attractive, red-haired woman sitting in the same corner of the pig pen Mac had so recently escaped from. She was bound like Mac had been and dressed in a mud-splattered dark grey pants suit.

Mac knew he was looking at the missing CIA agent's last moments of life.

The images that followed showed the pigs descending on her, biting into the woman's legs, hands, and feet as she struggled to push them away. Subsequent photos were no longer that of a living human being, but of a motionless corpse. The hogs were pictured fighting over the CIA agent's remains, eventually pulling her limbs off, and then finally ripping into her stomach until nothing but a bloodied patch of muddy dirt remained.

Mac whirled around at a sound coming from just behind him, his gun at the ready. He relaxed when he saw a large rat scurry into a corner of the room hidden in shadow. Then his eyes rested upon something he had missed earlier – the faint outline of a hidden door. The wall on the right side of the cellar had been painted white somewhat recently, absent much of the dirt and filth that covered the rest of the farmhouse. In the middle of that wall Mac saw the small gap between the wood that he was almost certain was another door.

He holstered his weapon and crossed the cellar floor and then lightly ran both his hands along the gap. That's when he realized light was coming from the other side of the wall, a much stronger light than the single bulb illuminating the cellar.

Mac pressed against the middle of what he believed to be a door, but the space didn't budge. He then pushed the right side and was met with the same unyielding resistance, but when the left side was pushed that part of the wall swung inward several inches. Mac could see the corner of another space that was no more than five or six feet deep. He pressed his left shoulder against the wall and pushed the door further open, allowing him to step into what appeared to be a large hidden closet.

A bright and buzzing florescent bulb hung from a set of small chains attached to the ceiling. Sitting on the dirt floor of the closet was a large four by four, locked metallic trunk. The lock was identical to the one that had been used to secure the cellar door allowing Mac to dispose of it in the very same way. His gun fired once and was then returned to its holster while Mac slowly and carefully pulled up the trunk lid.

What Mac discovered brought a wide smile to his face as his eyes lit up with unexpected excitement.

It appeared Christmas had arrived early…

7.

Ramtin Armeen sat in the back of the soft-leathered surroundings of his security enhanced slate black limousine and silently wondered if the Iranians were in fact monitoring his activity in Chicago. He had taken careful measures to try and move and then insulate as much of his business interests from Iranian influence, actions he knew would raise alarms within that government if discovered too soon.

That possibility was enough to force Armeen to travel to the farm outside Chicago to question the man who had apparently claimed that very thing to Hamid earlier in the day. It was a journey that left the billionaire increasingly annoyed with each passing mile as he considered simply calling ahead and telling the pig farmer to kill the stranger and be done with it.

Ah, but what if he has information that could be useful to me? What if it might help to further protect my Iranian holdings? Besides, I'm almost there. No sense turning back now.

Ramtin had not survived the myriad of challenges that was the Islamic dominated Iranian regime by ignoring potential threats. He had funneled millions in bribes over the last decade to ensure his business remained his own. If someone among the Supreme Leader's fawning cadre of sycophants intended to try and make an example of Ramtin, the billionaire would see that effort terminated sooner rather than later.

But what if Hamid is involved in the conspiracy as well? Perhaps he has taken offense that I don't share his own religious fervor?

It was not the first time Ramtin had considered that very possibility in recent months. He found Hamid's radicalism a useful tool to spread chaos and dissention across the globe, which in turn fed his burgeoning security business, but it was a quality the billionaire knew could also potentially turn against him if allowed to do so.

Ramtin Armeen knew the world was changing. The attack against the United States on September 11th, 2001 quickened the pace of that change and within that quickening was ample opportunity for those and others to profit both in money and more importantly, power. That potential power had led to a struggle between the great House of Saud and the Iranian-led Shi'a. The Saudis feared Iran's emerging nuclear program and were willing to pay handsomely for any information that could help them deter its continued growth. Ramtin had been playing both sides for the last two years, giving details (at a considerable price) to the Saudis while at the same time charging the Iranian government for his assistance in smoothing over the United Nations' ongoing nuclear inspections process.

It was during this time he had been given repeated assurances by figures within both the United Nations and the American government that his work was very much appreciated. A new world was emerging, one that would be absent silly religious disputes or national borders. Instead it would be a world dominated by absolute power and authority over others where a chosen few were to oversee the lesser masses. Ramtin was determined to make a place for himself near the head of that table.

The limo absorbed most of the bumps on the long and narrow dirt road that led to Allid Safarah's farm, but not all of them. Ramtin winced as the vehicle bounded over a particularly large dip in the road. He shook his head in disbelief that someone of his standing was actually making a journey in the muck and mud of rural Illinois. Few things disgusted him more than the seemingly endless and vast filth of the American countryside.

Ramtin glanced up to see the outline of his longtime driver and personal security detail through the dark-glassed partition. Abdul Arif had been a soldier in Saddam Hussein's elite Republican Guard combat brigade. Though a tribal Shia, Arif earned hard won respect as a fearless fighter during Iraq's almost nine year war against Shia-dominated Iran. The then young soldier rose quickly through the ranks of Saddam's military and was among the few Iraqis who remained near the Kuwait border and fought back against coalition forces during the Gulf War of the early 1990's. It was after that war that Abdul decided to visit family in Dubai, and it was there he met Ramtin Armeen at a nightclub. Two years later Armeen offered him a job providing security which, given the pay was nearly ten times that which he was earning in the Republican Guard, Abdul promptly accepted.

That was nearly a decade ago, and the forty-eight year old Abdul Arif had not left Ramtin Armeen's side since. And though the pay was excellent, Abdul would have happily done the job for free as he had fallen in love with Ramtin, a man the former Iraqi soldier considered both brilliant and beautiful.

Ramtin saw the farmhouse coming into view and then the multiple pig pens just beyond. It appeared a man who the billionaire assumed was Allid Safarah stood just outside one of the pens likely watching over the individual Hamid told him was Mac Walker, the one who said he was working with the Iranian government.

Well, Mr. Walker, I will confirm that claim to be true or not, and you will soon be dead regardless.

Ramtin lowered the limo's glass partition.

"Drive past the house and park near the pens."

The billionaire glanced at Allid's home, shocked that a human being could live in a place of such disrepair, surrounded by so much dirt and mud, and strangely aggressive open space.

The limo came to a stop forty feet from where Allid stood with his back to the vehicle. The farmer's refusal to even turn around annoyed Ramtin, a man unaccustomed to being so ignored.

Perhaps I'll leave here having killed him too.

It wasn't an idle thought. Ramtin Armeen held little value for any life beyond his own. He knew that by tomorrow the world would be both horrified and mesmerized by the reports of mass casualties in locations throughout the United States. The media would dutifully broadcast and re-broadcast the bloodied remains of countless children and the underlying and undeniable message to all of America would be *none of you are safe.*

People would demand they be protected. The government would promise to do so, and that thirst for power and authority would then necessitate an approach well beyond the borders of the United States. The demand for more safety would have to be a global effort, and there Ramtin would find his greatest opportunity. The epicenter for this effort had already been hatched in Chicago and would soon spread throughout America and then beyond. He would continue to work with both the Saudis and the Iranians, all the while improving his own standing, wealth, and influence.

If thousands of children were to die to ensure that conclusion, so be it. The world had become too crowded anyways. The planet's long term health required men like him to outline acceptable behaviors for everyone else. Those who refused the necessary mandates would simply no longer be allowed to exist at all.

The billionaire was so engrossed in his own plans for the future his awareness of the present suffered terribly. Ramtin had stepped out of the limo and didn't immediately notice that the man he thought to be Allid Safarah was actually just an empty jacket hanging from a post. His driver and bodyguard had noticed though. Abdul's gun was already drawn as he instinctively moved to push Ramtin back into the limousine.

"What is going on?"

Ramtin's question wasn't answered by his bodyguard. Instead both men looked toward the small covered porch of the farmhouse. It was there Ramtin received his answer, an answer that caused the man who hoped to one day rule much of the world to be reminded he was just a man after all, and more than capable of meeting the same death he intended to visit upon so many others.

"This can't be."

8.

Mac Walker was delighted to have found Allid's weapons stash in the hidden room of the farmhouse cellar. He was particularly pleased to be able to point a fully functional, albeit older model, Iranian-made shoulder-launched RPG-7 at the black limousine as it crept toward the pig pens.

Mac waited just behind the farthest corner of the home's covered porch and was even more impressed at the sight of two men exiting the vehicle.

That's Ramtin Armeen himself!

Mac's eyes narrowed as he tried to get a better look at the limousine driver, hoping to confirm it was Hamid Gilani. Having both men in front of the RPG-7 would bring a swift and decisive end to his current assignment, and hopefully then save a great many lives in the process.

But that's not Hamid.

At the very moment Mac's mind formed that statement both Ramtin Armeen and Abdul Arif looked up and then directly at, Mac Walker. The Project Icon operative hesitated for a half second as he noted the limousine driver was armed before Mac pulled the RPG's trigger.

The rocket propelled grenade unleashed a loud whoosh as Mac braced himself to avoid being pushed over by the force of the rocket's booster propellant activating. Mac knew as soon as the weapon fired his aim was as accurate as he would have hoped. The rocket arced across the property followed by a thin trail of black-grey smoke before detonating just under the vehicle's rear quarter panel.

Normally such a blast would have lifted a car several inches off of the ground, but Ramtin's heavily fortified, armor plated blast resistant limousine merely groaned from deep within its metal frame.

Mac dropped the RPG and picked up the 1970's era Chinese made AK-47 that he had also taken from the pig farmer's small but impressive collection. His keen eyes scanned the space between the farmhouse and the limousine, looking for any sign of movement. It appeared a shoe was sticking out the back of the half-open passenger door, but Mac was unable to locate the second man.

The pigs, frightened by the RPG detonation, were shrieking loudly.

I'll huff, and I'll puff, and I'll blow you jihadi scum to kingdom come...

The shoe inside the limo moved slowly from side to side, indicating whoever was inside, and Mac had already assumed it was Ramtin Armeen, remained alive.

The driver reacted quick – real quick. That indicates some kind of specialist training. He managed to push Armeen back into the car, and then somehow disappear. Maybe he's in the limo too waiting to shoot my face off if I try and take a peek inside.

Mac wished for another grenade to place into the RPG, but he had found only the one. The AK-47 and its 30-round magazine would have to do. Keeping his eyes locked onto the limousine's partially open passenger door, he made his way carefully down the porch steps and toward the parked vehicle.

As he came within twenty feet of the limo, Mac fell into a crouch so he could glance under the car to see if the second man was hiding on the other side. Finding nothing, he stood back up and continued walking toward the vehicle.

Just as Mac Walker stood back up, Abdul Arif silently repositioned himself near the front right wheel he remained hidden behind. He thought he could hear Ramtin breathing from inside the limo and hoped the billionaire had been protected from the brunt of the RPG blast. As for Abdul himself, he had escaped injury almost entirely after diving underneath the bottom of the heavily fortified car and then crawling to the other side.

Abdul had no idea who the man was that fired from the farmhouse porch. He only knew it was his job to see that man dead and Ramtin Armeen returned to safety. The former Iraqi Republican Guard officer intended to do just that. Abdul could hear the other man's footsteps getting closer. He held his breath, grateful for the familiar weight of the Tariq nine-millimeter pistol in his right hand. It was a weapon that had served him well for many years, and Abdul was confident it would do so once again.

Mac peered into the limo's backseat and confirmed it was in fact Ramtin Armeen who lay inside on his back. Mac could see the billionaire's chest raising and lowering, indicating he was still alive.

That just leaves the other guy. Now where the hell did he go?

The front seat appeared empty. Mac shook his head as his eyes scanned the pig pens, increasingly confused as to how a man could seemingly disappear.

Normally in combat, by the time one sees their enemy, it is too late. The best soldier develops the inherent ability to sense danger before that danger actually and fully manifests itself. It was the split second difference between death or continued survival.

Mac caught a flash of movement to his left and instinctively knew it was the second man he had been looking for. He also realized he didn't have time to raise the AK-47 and fire before the other man did the same with his own weapon.

Damn.

Abdul's first shot missed no more than an inch beyond Mac's left ear. The air literally sizzled as the bullet flew past. Mac instantly dropped to his knees, seeking refuge behind the limousine's front left side as he pointed the AK-47 in front of him and unleashed a burst of semi-automatic fire that he knew would keep the other man from moving himself entirely to Mac's side of the vehicle.

The momentary stalemate meant to provide Mac time to reassess his situation and come with up with a viable solution that ended with the other man dead. Abdul had no intention of giving the Project Icon operative that time though. Instead the former Iraqi soldier crouched and then catapulted himself gracefully past the limo's hood as he fired his weapon in the location he thought Mac to be.

He thought wrong.

Mac had already managed to crawl under the limo. From that vantage point he was able to watch Abdul leap out from in front of the car's hood and fire off two well placed rounds into the very space Mac had just seconds earlier been crouching. It was then Mac who fired the AK-47, holding it sideways and spraying the ground where Abdul gracefully landed. The first two bullets missed wide right, but the next two found his upper left shoulder, spinning the Iraqi around as he cried out in shocked pain.

Even as Mac squeezed off three more rounds he was impressed by the former Iraqi soldier's skill and determination. In his long military career, Mac Walker had certainly come up against far less capable fighters.

Abdul Arif's body was still, the result of one of the AK-47's bullets tearing through his brain stem. Mac pushed himself out from underneath the car and carefully walked up to the body to make certain Abdul was dead. After doing so he turned his full attention to Ramtin Armeen who remained lying on his back in the limo's backseat.

"Can you move?"

Ramtin's only response was a pained moan.

Mac made certain the Iranian billionaire wasn't armed and then grabbed him by the front of his custom made suit jacket and pulled him out of the car and propped him up against the rear wheel, a displacement that caused Ramtin to gasp in pain.

While the security modified car door had shielded the billionaire from most of the RPG blast's impact, he still suffered from a concussion and two broken ribs that made it difficult for him to breathe.

"Where's your phone?"

Ramtin's eyes opened, though it took several seconds before they were able to focus more clearly on Mac.

"In my jacket."

Mac kept the AK-47 pointed at the billionaire.

"Get it out and see if it's still working."

Ramtin did as he was told, wincing from the pain of moving his right hand into the interior pocket of his suit. The phone emerged looking unscathed.

"Yes, it's still working."

Mac nodded.

"Good, now listen to me very carefully, Mr. Armeen. You are going to call off whatever attack you have planned. The school shootings, the daycare centers, call it off now – *all of it*. Do that, and I won't shoot you dead here in the dirt."

Ramtin grimaced, though his eyes indicated hope he might yet make it out of this mess alive.

"I am not responsible for the logistics. I don't know---"

Mac fired a single bullet into the space between Ramtin's legs, missing his manhood by no more than a few inches.

"I don't want to hear that bullshit, Mr. Armeen. A businessman like you, there's no way you leave anything to chance. Take that phone and call off the terror cell operatives, and do it now. Perhaps start with Hamid Gilani."

The billionaire grunted, amused at Mac's suggestion Hamid would be open to considering such an order.

"Gilani won't stop. He's a zealot, he won't *ever* stop. Perhaps I can help with the others though, but I need one thing first."

Mac's eyes narrowed as he prepared to fire another round off.

"What's that?"

Ramtin cleared his throat, growing more comfortable and confident at the prospect of being able to negotiate.

"I want my attorney present before I make those calls. He will be my witness that this is being done under duress, and without my admitting to being part of any alleged attacks."

Mac was stunned by Ramtin's belief he could make such a demand even as the body of his just-deceased driver lay no more than ten feet from him. It seemed every one of these jihadis had a natural instinct to immediately lawyer up when caught.

"Are you kidding me?"

The billionaire straightened his tie, and then proceeded to cough up a sizeable amount of froth-tinged blood.

"I assure you, I am not."

Mac pointed to the fresh blood on Ramtin's hands.

"That blood there is from your lungs, understand? That means your shit is seriously messed up. You might have no more than an hour of life left in you, less if I decide you're not cooperating and not worth the time, effort, and expense of calling you an ambulance."

Ramtin refused to admit he had little leverage to negotiate. Instead he decided to emphasize the importance of the information he could provide, and the many lives that were still at terrible risk.

"You need me, Mr. Walker. I can allow you to play the part of hero. Isn't that what you types are always hoping for? To do that, I want protection for myself in the form of my personal attorney. This is America is it not? Am I not innocent until proven guilty?"

Mac had to force himself not pull the trigger, so sickened was he by the preening billionaire's infuriating confidence that he would buy his way out of his current crisis.

"How do I know you even have the information to stop this on your phone?"

Ramtin appeared genuinely offended by the accusation.

"I have no reason to lie. You're the one with the gun. Here, I'll make a call to show prove I can be trusted."

Mac issued a growled warning.

"You make that call in English. I hear one Allahu Akbar and I swear I'm putting a bullet between your eyes."

The billionaire nodded.

"Of course, Mr. Walker, of course."

Mac watched as Ramtin speed dialed a number and then put the cell phone to his right ear.

"This is me. Yes, it's me. Terminate the operation. No, there is no need to confirm with Mr. Gilani. He can no longer be trusted. I am ordering you to terminate, do you understand? Good, thank you."

Ramtin ended the call and looked up at Mac with a sneering smile.

"See? I am a man of my word, Mr. Walker. If you wish for me to make the other calls, I am to have my attorney present when I do so."

Mac lowered the AK-47.

"So you're certain you have all the contact numbers in that phone of yours?"

The billionaire rolled his eyes, appearing utterly bored by Mac's ongoing questions."

"Of course, you said yourself I'm not a businessman who would leave things to chance."

It was Mac Walker who then smiled.

"Good."

Mac lifted the AK-47 upward before sending the butt end of the assault rifle crashing into Ramtin Armeen's forehead, knocking him out. Mac then reached down and retrieved the billionaire's phone and pressed the redial button. The call rang twice before an agitated male voice with a deep Middle Eastern accent picked up.

"Yes, Mr. Armeen, we are terminating. You should not be calling me again!"

Mac's smile widened as he ended the call without saying anything.

Well I'll be damned the lying bastard was telling the truth!

9.

The next call Mac made on Ramtin's phone was to Tilley. He told the Project Icon supervisor he had taken the Iranian billionaire alive, but was at the moment unable to locate Hamid Gilani. When Tilley heard Mac had made Ramtin call off one of the terror cells, and that the other terror cell contacts were saved on the billionaire's phone, Tilley made clear his gratitude to Mac.

"I've already given the FBI the heads up, Mac. Ramtin Armeen will be taken into custody, and the Feds will use the contact numbers to sweep the terror cell locations. You did real good."

Mac glanced toward the pigs that had returned to happily munching on Allid Safarah's body. He didn't share Tilley's optimism. So long as a man remained out there somewhere who was as dangerously motivated to inflict harm upon others as was Hamid Gilani, the assignment was not complete.

"We still have to take care of Gilani."

"I agree, Mac, and we will. We have all the local, state and federal agencies on alert. We'll get him too. After you hand off Ramtin and his phone, why don't you go back to the safe house and relax? I'll update you as soon as I hear anything on Gilani. You get some rest and I'll be briefing the senator on today's developments."

Ramtin Armeen began to stir where he sat propped up against the side of the limo.

"What's gonna happen to Ramtin? I thought the senator didn't want to risk him lawyering up on us?"

Mac could hear Tilley's smile pressing against his phone.

"Oh, I don't think we need to worry about Armeen manipulating the benefits of the U.S. legal system. We have other options on what to do after we get every bit of terrorist-related information we can pull out of him."

Mac looked up at the sound of an approaching helicopter.

"Guess they took your heads-up pretty serious, Ray. They sent a chopper out here already."

Tilley had to shout so Mac could hear him over the din of the helicopter.

"That would be someone from the FBI branch in Chicago. They know to keep this quiet until we've had a chance to interrogate Ramtin. While that's happening their tech department will be extracting all the information from that phone. I'd estimate we'll have every one of those terror cells locked down by the end of the day. I'm pretty sure you just helped us to save a hell of a lot of lives, Mac – most of them kids. Like I said, get some rest and I'll be in contact again soon."

Ten minutes later found Mac Walker staring down at the outskirts of Chicago through a window of a FBI helicopter as it made its way toward a rooftop helipad atop the Bureau's Chicago office. Upon exiting the chopper Mac was greeted by an attractive black female in her late thirties dressed in grey slacks and a dark blue fleece jacket who handed him another shadow cell to replace the one destroyed at the pig farm.

"Mr. Walker, just to be clear, we never met today. You were never here. Mr. Tilley was very specific in his instructions. Please follow me. I'm going to have you exit the building from a utility service tunnel that will take you across the street, understood?"

Mac merely nodded, appreciating the woman's to-the-point demeanor and professionalism. He followed her down several flights of stairs and then through a door where he found himself standing in a vast, underground parking garage.

"Right this way, Mr. Walker. Please stay close to the wall to avoid the security monitors."

Mac did as he was told. He was taken to a white metallic door in the far left corner of the garage. The FBI agent input a code onto a digital keypad and then pulled the door open, motioning for Mac to step into the narrow concrete passage beyond.

"It's less than a hundred yards to the other side of the street. The door opens out into an empty alleyway. From there I assume you already know where you intend to go?"

Mac shrugged and then walked into the tunnel.

"Yeah, I'm good."

Before she closed the door behind him, the FBI agent looked up at Mac and then took his right hand into her own and shook it firmly.

"It's an honor to meet you, Mr. Walker. Thank you for what you've done for the country, and please be careful. Oh, and one more thing, you'll definitely want to clean yourself up. You smell like Satan's ass."

The door closed leaving Mac alone in the tunnel. He tilted his head downward until his nose brushed up against his left forearm and then he inhaled and was promptly greeted by the reality of what the FBI agent suggested.

Whew!

A shower and change of clothes was definitely in order.

9:20 p.m.

Mac awoke to the sound of his newly received shadow cell. He had returned to the safe house by cab, quickly taken a shower, and then decided to lie down for what he intended to be a short nap. That had been almost five hours ago.

"You still in Chicago, Mac?"

Tilley sounded upbeat and rested - a stark contrast to Mac's own struggling to wake senses.

"Uh, yeah…figure I'll fly back to Louisiana tomorrow morning."

"Just wanted you to know we got a line on Gilani. An image grabbed from a rest area camera off Highway 31 in Northern Michigan appears to be him. Looks like he's planning on trying to cross into Canada. Feds have an entire detail on their way to the area. Thought you'd like to know."

Mac wiped the sleep from his eyes with his left hand while holding the phone up to his ear with his right.

"Yeah, that's good news, Ray."

"Oh, and we've already shut down over twenty of the terror cells and I was informed about ten minutes ago two more are turning themselves in. These guys were armed to the teeth, Mac. We found the list of the targets. It's just as we suspected, a bunch of schools, a few college campuses, and some daycare centers. The public won't even know about it - just another almost disaster that was avoided. It all came together so well, you're gonna get a lot of work after this. The senator is particularly happy to have Project Icon available to him."

Mac stood up from the bed and looked out the window at the bustling traffic below. He watched a laughing couple exit Uncle Chan's across the street and suddenly remembered his promised 10:00 dinner with Li's family in their home above the restaurant, a memory that caused Mac's stomach to growl its own reminder he hadn't eaten anything since morning.

"Hey, Ray, I gotta go grab a bite - just realized I'm starving."

Ray Tilley chuckled.

"You bet, Mac, and have a safe trip home."

Mac put the shadow cell down on the narrow kitchen counter and then began to put on a fresh change of clothes. All he had left in the apartment that was clean was a white t-shirt, blue jeans, and a pair of reasonably clean white running shoes. His sidearm and shoulder holster were slung over a chair next to the bed. Without a jacket to wear he had nothing in which to conceal his weapon. He certainly wasn't going to wear his pig-mud drenched windbreaker to dinner.

Then again, the idea of going anywhere without his weapon was not something Mac Walker was willing to entertain either.

What to do, what to do...

Mac glanced at his watch and saw it was just past 9:30. Punctuality had long ago been instilled in him by his parents, and even more during his time in the military. He had no intention of showing up late to dinner with Li's family. The food was bound to be good, and as for Li, Mac hoped she might prove interested in getting to know him a little better as well.

The increasingly hungry Project Icon operative jammed his SIG P226 into the back of his pants, held the shoulder holster in his left hand, and made his way to the door. As his hand reached out to unlock the deadbolt he paused, instinctively wondering if Tilley could have been wrong about Gilani making his way north through Michigan.

Mac reached back and withdrew his handgun and turned off the apartment's lights. He then returned to the window and scanned both sides of the street looking for anything, or anyone that struck him as out of place.

Having confirmed as best he could no-one was waiting to ambush him, Mac moved himself back to the door and unlocked it, gun held ready, and then opened the door halfway. He was relieved to find nobody waiting on the other side to kick the door in, or take a shot at him. Mac stepped out onto the stairs and peered into the gloom of the empty alleyway below. The only thing to be found was the rental car parked in the very same space as it had been when Gilani had taken an iron bar to his head which initiated the unexpected field trip to pig farm hell.

Mac locked the door behind him and then bound down the stairs, keeping himself low as his eyes continued to scan the area around him. He then made is way to the sidewalk and stopped a young Asian teenager dressed in an oversized red satin Chicago Bulls athletic jacket.

"Hey, you speak English?"

The teenager paused, his face a mix of fear and uncertainty.

"Yeah, why?"

"I'll give you a hundred dollars for your jacket."

The young man's eyes widened slightly. Mac had his full attention.

"You have the cash on you?"

Mac took out a roll of bills from the front pocket of his jeans.

"Yeah, so we have a deal?"

The teen glanced at the money and then looked back up at Mac.

"Two hundred."

Mac was about to protest but his determination not to be late for dinner pushed aside his certainty the kid was squeezing him.

"Fine, I'll give you two hundred. That thing better not smell like smoke."

The Asian shook his head as he began to remove the jacket.

"I don't smoke and this thing is almost new! You a tourist or something?"

Mac took the jacket and then gave the teenager the two hundred dollars.

"No, just a guy on his way to dinner."

The kid took the money and then was off, likely wanting to hurry away before Mac changed his mind. Mac strapped his shoulder holster on, holstered his weapon, and then zipped the front of the jacket halfway up, happy to find it was an almost perfect fit.

His stomach growled again as the smells from Uncle Chan's wafted across the street. Mac caught a flash of motion from the second floor of the restaurant building and looked up to see Li waving happily down at him.

"I'll come down and let you in! Dinner is almost ready!"

Mac waved back and then made his way quickly across the street. When he reached the other side he stopped to look behind him, certain he was being watched.

His hand reached toward the holstered SIG as he thought he saw something move in the darkness of the alley just behind the parked rental car. A large truck rumbled down the crowded street, momentarily blocking Mac's view of the alley.

By the time the truck passed by, whoever might have been in the alley was gone.

If anything was even there at all.

Mac heard Li unlocking the restaurant door behind him. He turned and was greeted by her wide, friendly smile. She wore a knee-length cream colored dress that fit snugly over a firm, compact body. Her dark hair was tied back in a pony tail that, when combined with her porcelain-smooth skin, made her appear barely old enough to drink.

"I was worried you would forget! Grandmother is looking forward to meeting you! I hope you are hungry!"

Mac offered his host a quick half smile as he nodded.

"Actually, I'm starving."

Li had Mac follow her into the near darkness of the closed for the night restaurant and then toward the kitchen area in the back where a door stood open inside of which was a dimly lit staircase leading to the second floor. Before heading up the stairs she turned to face Mac, her voice suggesting a hint of shyness.

"My family has never invited a customer upstairs to eat in our home, but after the great favor you did for us, they are honored to have you as their guest. *I* am honored to have you as our guest."

Mac lifted his nose upward and took a deep breath, inhaling the multiple flavors of the excellent meal that awaited him upstairs.

"I just try and do what needs to be done, Li. Can't say I always get it right, but I do try."

Li found herself staring at the intensity that flickered within Mac's eyes before she quickly looked down, embarrassed Mac might have noticed. Unfortunately her eyes came to rest on another area of Mac's blue jean clad form, which caused her even greater panic.

"Uh, right this way."

Mac Walker suppressed a smile as he noted how flustered Li had become. That is, until he found himself staring at her backside at the very moment Li turned around and caught him doing so.

Li was on the step above Mac so their faces were nearly even as she turned all the way around to face him. The right corner of her mouth curled upward into a slight grin just before she took Mac's face in both of her hands and pulled him closer. Her lips initially just brushed lightly against his before they parted and then returned to kiss him with much greater force and urgency, a gesture Mac happily returned in kind.

Li's eyebrows raised slightly above her dark eyes, conveying her appreciation for Mac's willingness to accommodate her desire to kiss him, something she had wanted to do the moment he had saved her from the frightening confrontation with the violent customer the previous day.

"I am very glad there are still men like you who try to get it right, Mac."

10.

The upstairs apartment that was home to Li and her family was an eclectic mix of well organized chaos. The walls were covered in family photos and an assortment of heirlooms sat atop tables and desks throughout the space. Though somewhat cramped, Mac immediately sensed it to be a place filled with love, a testament to the likely challenging journey that had taken the family from China to the United States.

Mac was re-introduced to Li's father Charlie Yang and her mother Lin. Charlie was nearly sixty, while Lin was not yet fifty. Both had faces that bore the deep lines of hardship and toil, but their eyes happily reflected the kindness and hope so common to American immigrants who had come to love the country that had taken them in and granted such generous opportunity.

Li motioned for Mac to follow her toward the kitchen where a white haired old woman dressed in an oversized blue sweatshirt and tan khaki slacks sat watching him carefully with heavy lidded eyes and the faintest of smiles on skin that appeared as thin and dry as parchment paper.

"Mac, this is my grandmother, Ping. She turned eighty-six last month."

The grandmother rose from her chair and though she shared the same bent back as her son and was considerably older, she moved with a confident quickness that belied her many years.

Both Li and Mac listened as the old woman pointed to Mac while saying something in her native tongue to her granddaughter. Li turned and smiled to Mac.

"She would be honored to give you a reading, Mac. In China she made a little money telling fortunes on the streets of Lhasa. People continue to see her here as well for a reading from time to time. It is considered a great honor for her to make you this offer."

Li's parents had gathered behind their daughter and were looking up at Mac as well, clearly hoping he would agree. Mac Walker considered such things as fortunes and organized religion to be little more than mumbo-jumbo meant to make people feel better about things they could never hope to understand, but not wanting to offend Li's family, especially her grandmother, he nodded his head.

"Sure, why not?"

Li's father began nodding his head as well, speaking in heavily accented English.

"Good, good. I will get you a chair."

The old woman returned to her own chair and waited patiently for Mac to take his place directly in front of her. Charlie pushed a black wooden chair behind him and then motioned for Mac to sit.

Li's grandmother stared silently into Mac's eyes for several seconds before lifting her hands toward him with the palms facing up. Mac glanced at Li, wondering what he was supposed to do next. Li gave him a reassuring smile.

"She is asking permission to touch your face, Mac. That is how she does her readings."

Mac looked back at the old woman and shrugged.

"Yeah, that's fine, though I doubt you'll get much from this mug other than the fact I've had my nose broken about ten too many times."

Grandma Ping ignored Mac's attempt at humor, instead leaning forward and taking his face into her delicate, aged fingers as she closed her eyes and took a slow, deep breath. Her hands moved slowly along his jaw line, paused for a moment at his temples, and then the fingers of her right hand traced the wrinkles of Mac's brow while Ping's left hand brushed down gently over his nose.

Mac found the sensation oddly comforting. His muscles relaxed as he closed his eyes while the old woman's hands continued to move slowly over the contours of his face. This went on for nearly two more minutes before Ping withdrew from Mac and then sat staring at him with that same almost-smile she wore when he had first arrived inside her home.

Ping began to speak in her native tongue, occasionally pointing to Mac for emphasis. Mac looked up at Li who was carefully listening to her grandmother to be certain she understood each word correctly.

"She says you are the protector and a good man, though often troubled by regret. You are afraid of the bad in this world that you cannot stop. You want nothing more than to be left alone, but feel an obligation to help others because it's what you do best. You yearn to be normal, but know that such a life will never be yours."

As Li continued to interpret her grandmother's reading, Mac's eyes fell to the old woman and found her staring back at him with a particularly urgent intensity. Her dark eyes appeared to reflect the emotions she spoke of back to Mac, primarily those of sadness, regret, and uncertainty.

"You will come to know even greater challenge as many more place themselves in your care. When it is coldest, your determination will burn hottest. The sky above grows dark with death, but you will not be defeated. Where others fall, the Walker will yet remain."

Mac stiffened at the mention of his last name – a name he had not shared with Li or her family, and certainly should not have been known to the old woman.

Ping smiled at Mac and then lifted her right hand to caress his cheek once more while her voice whispered the last of her reading.

"She is honored to have the protector in our home, especially with such a terrible threat so close at hand."

Both Mac and Li frowned at the same time as they wondered what threat Ping spoke of. Mac watched the old woman look past him toward the apartment entrance and saw the reflections of three men within Ping's eyes staring back at him.

A familiar voice hissed out an ominous warning.

"You all get on the floor, face down. Anyone try anything, and I swear to god I'll blow every one of your damn heads off. That especially goes for you, white boy."

Tyrell Watts, the young man Mac had recently designated *a hood-rat*, had returned, his common sense over-run by having been so disgraced by someone who dared stand up to his aggressive bullying threats. He was joined by two other men of similar age, all dressed in the city streets-approved fashion of large sweatshirts and laughably sagging jeans.

"That's the guy who kicked your ass?"

The largest of the three young black men, standing six foot five and weighing nearly three hundred pounds, was looking at Mac incredulously, unable to comprehend the idea of Mac overpowering Tyrell.

"He didn't kick my ass! Got lucky is all. Now I'm here to make it right."

Hood-rat's right hand gripped a handgun which he raised and pointed at Mac, who in turn noted it was shaking slightly in the younger man's hand.

"I said on your knees."

Mac Walker shook his head slowly as his voice crept back to the three men without a hint of concern that he was so clearly outnumbered.

"No."

Hood-rat leered at his two seemingly like-minded companions.

"See, guy is crazy, thinks he's in some kind of Rambo movie or somethin'."

"Shut your mouth, hood-rat. I'm talking to this big fella."

The eyes of the largest of the three widened as he looked at Mac and then back to Tyrell.

"Tyrell, he just call you hood-rat? What the---?"

Mac took a slow step forward with both his hands raised chest high.

"You boys don't need to be doing this. I don't want to hurt you, ok?"

Mac kept his eyes on the largest of the three men who he determined was the leader, while at the same time pointing to Tyrell.

"Your friend there deserved every bit of what he got. He came into these fine people's place of business and started cursing them out, making threats, basically acting the fool. I could have killed him then if I wanted to, but instead put him in a cab and sent him on his way. Now why in the hell did you let yourself be talked into coming back here to…hell, I don't even know why. To rob this family? To try and take me out? Really? Is all that worth doing because he had his pride hurt? If he was a real man, wouldn't he have come back here alone? Why drag you two into this?"

The larger of the three glanced at his two companions and then grunted back at Mac.

"We got our boy's back. Can't have people disrespecting and getting away with it."

Mac took another step toward the men, keeping his hands up by his sides as he did so.

"These people didn't disrespect Tyrell. If you have a complaint with me, fine, but leave this family out of it. How did you get in here, anyway?"

Tyrell rolled his eyes at Mac, growing impatient with the conversation.

"Back door was open. You think we're too dumb to know how to open a door?"

Li was shaking her head while turning it so she could look up at Mac.

"I locked that door myself."

Li's comment further agitated Tyrell, causing him to point his weapon down at her.

"See? She don't like our kind! Now she's calling us liars. See why I was so upset?"

Mac ignored Tyrell, keeping his eyes on the man in the middle.

"My name is Mac, what's yours?"

The black man's eyes narrowed as he tried to figure out what Mac was really trying to ask him.

"I'm just asking your name so we can talk like men. I have a proposition that I hope will keep any of you from getting hurt."

"Call me Rip. What kind of deal you getting at?"

Mac gave a hard stare at Tyrell, his eyes warning the hood-rat to keep his trigger finger from unwisely transforming a tense discussion into a violent altercation, and then Mac's focus returned to Rip.

"Nice to meet you, Rip. It's real simple, actually. I'll give you a thousand dollars for your trouble. A thousand dollars for you to turn around and get the hell out of here and never bother these people again."

Rip's mouth turned downward as he considered the possibility of Mac lying.

"A thousand dollars? Why would you do that?"

Tyrell shook his head angrily and took two quick steps toward Mac with his gun pointed at the Project Icon operative's head.

"I ain't listening to this bullshit! Get on your knees!"

Mac almost felt sorry for Tyrell's repeated error of getting too close to him. It was the same mistake he had made in the restaurant that left him choked out in the span of a few seconds. Mac also made certain that if Tyrell was able to actually fire a shot, the bullet would miss high and right of where Li's family lay on the apartment floor.

With a subtle flick of his left hand that he knew would give him the half second distraction he needed, Mac Walker's right hand struck like a coiled cobra catching a nerve just under Tyrell's right wrist that caused the younger man's fingers to open and the gun to fall from his grasp.

Mac then turned and caught the gun with his left hand while simultaneously removing his own SIG P226 with his right hand leaving him pointing both weapons at the three intruders while standing far enough behind Tyrell to provide Mac cover should the other two men try and fire upon him.

Rip's mouth fell open as he grappled with the seeming impossibility of watching a human being move so fast. The third man was also staring at Mac in amazement, momentarily lowering his own weapon.

'That was some Bruce Lee shit! Who is this guy?"

Mac pointed the two guns he held toward the floor, hoping to prove he didn't want to hurt anyone so long as the three men simply turned around and left.

"I'm just someone who's trying to avoid a confrontation. This family, these people, they don't deserve this kind of trouble. America has enough assholes out there trying to kill every one of us. Why do we seem so damned intent on killing ourselves too?"

Tyrell turned to Rip while he pointed at Mac.

"Shoot this fool dead, man!"

Mac knew then that Rip didn't want to actually kill anyone. He might have been some wanna-be thug, but he wasn't a killer.

"Hey, you a soldier?"

Mac nodded.

"I was, yeah. How about you?"

Rip shook his head.

"No, not me, but my gramps was – Vietnam. He's got the cancer now. Says it's from all that Agent Orange they dumped on him over there."

Mac knew the story all too well. Agent Orange was an herbicidal program initiated by President Kennedy to clear some of the more heavily forested areas in and around the North and South Vietnamese border. The theory was it would make it more difficult for the communists to hide out near the DMZ. While it killed thousands of acres of jungle foliage, it also likely contributed to both short and long term health problems for the Vietnamese and American soldiers who came in contact with the powerful chemical agent. Mac had long considered the U.S. government's refusal to accept any responsibility for the damage Agent Orange might have caused its own soldiers to be among that war's greatest crimes.

"I'm sorry about your grandfather's illness. That was a tough war, ultimately made worse because the soldiers weren't simply allowed to win it."

Rip sensed Mac's sympathy to be genuine. He shook his head, his eyes full of shame.

"We outta here. This was a stupid-ass idea. Sorry for scaring you all."

Despite the dark hue of his skin, Tyrell's face managed to turn red.

"What? No way, man! At least get his money!"

Rip turned to Tyrell, giving the smaller man a look that let him know he wasn't in the mood to listen to complaint.

"We shouldn't even be here. The man is right, these people don't deserve this. Now shut your mouth and let's go."

Mac holstered his own weapon while putting Tyrell's gun on a table behind him,

"Wait, hold on a second. I have fourteen hundred dollars on me. I want you to take it, do something nice for your grandpa. What's his name?"

Rip turned around and looked down at the floor, mumbling the name as if the shame he felt made him unworthy to speak it.

"Josiah Meeks."

Mac removed his money roll and was double-checking that the amount was correct.

"Do you know the branch he served in?"

Rip cleared his throat as his eyes remained fixed upon the floor.

"It was the Army. He was a staff sergeant."

Mac waited for Rip's eyes to rise so he could look into them directly. When they finally did, he placed the money into Rip's right hand.

"I'd like you to do me a favor. You tell Staff Sergeant Meeks thank you for his service, and get him something nice with this money, ok?"

Rip's eyes were wet with approaching tears he struggled to hold back. He shook his head while again clearing his throat.

"Yeah, I'm gonna do that. First thing…"

Mac Walker watched the three would-be intruders turn around and leave. Of all the potentially deadly encounters during a life of bullets and blood, it was perhaps his most gratifying conclusion yet as it proved itself to be a crisis averted. The fact it cost him some of his assignment money was a price he was more than willing to pay to spare lives that still had hope for greater potential.

"Is it safe to get up?"

Mac turned to look at Li and nodded.

"Yeah, it's safe. They won't be back."

Within minutes Mac sat with Li and her family making quick work of plates of some of the most delicious food he had ever been served. There was laughter, love, and friendship, a taste of life Mac had for too long been unfamiliar with.

Finally Mac sat back in his chair and waved away offers of more food.

"No, I'm done for. Every bit of it was amazing – thank you."

Li looked at Mac warmly, her eyes holding his for a moment before she looked to her grandmother.

"You were right, Grandmother, Mac *is* the protector."

Li was interrupted by the sound of Mac's shadow cell. Mac quickly apologized and then indicated he needed to take the call. He stood up from the table and walked to the apartment's double window that offered a view of the Chinatown neighborhood outside.

"I'm here, go ahead."

Tilley's tone indicated he was back in stress mode.

"It wasn't him, Mac. We think the guy in Michigan was a decoy but he's not talking. As of now, we have no idea where Gilani is. You need to watch your back and get the hell out of Chicago ASAP."

Mac felt a chill go up his spine as he instinctively replayed something indicated to him earlier that he knew he should have given more attention to.

"Will do, Ray. Talk to you soon."

Mac placed his cell phone back into his jacket and looked across the room at Li's grandmother who was at that time, staring back at him as if fully expecting the question to come.

"Li, please ask your grandmother if those three men here earlier were the terrible threat she said was so close at hand."

Mac waited as Li posed the question, even as he already knew the answer. He watched the old woman's mouth curl downward into a pronounced frown as she shook her head no. Mac recalled Li's earlier confusion as to how the men had entered the building through an open back door – a door Li was certain she had earlier locked herself.

Gilani.

11.

"Keep your hands where I can see them, Walker."

Inside his own head, Mac Walker was raging at himself for having been caught so unaware so easily.

I've put these people in terrible danger.

"Put your weapon on the floor and kick it over to me, please."

Mac did as he was told but not before quickly applying the weapon's modified safety, all the while keeping his eyes fixated on Hamid Gilani. The Muslim terrorist was dressed in a tattered blue baseball cap, dark denim jacket, and khaki slacks. In his right hand he held a Glock 26, a weapon that if fully loaded Mac knew had a ten round capacity plus possibly another in the chamber.

Gilani leaned down slowly to pick up Mac's SIG which he then stuffed into the back of his jeans.

"This is the second time I've taken your gun from you."

Mac stood silently with his hands raised even as he calculated as many options as possible to ensure Li's family remained alive while Gilani was given the death he so richly deserved.

"Are these your friends, Walker?"

Mac's jaw clenched as he answered between gritted teeth.

"Yes, they are, and you're going to leave them the hell alone. This is between you and me, Hamid – *not them*."

Gilani offered a sly half smile as his eyes gleamed with the belief he held a clear advantage over the former Navy SEAL.

"On the contrary, if you care about them, then all the more reason I allow you to see them killed. I want you to know this family died because of *you*. I want that to be your last thought. None of this is over until I say it's over, and I have no intention of doing that until America finally begins paying for its many sins, starting with the blood of its children turning the streets red."

He still intends to attack a school.

"You talk too much."

Hamid's eyes narrowed as he pointed back at Mac with his gun.

"What?"

"I said you talk too much. It's the same thing with you kill-for-Allah types, always making threats, speeches…all that bullshit."

Gilani was less than pleased to see so little fear in Mac Walker's eyes. He looked past the Project Icon operative and found the large and far less confident eyes of Li staring back at him.

"*You*, come here."

Mac moved a step closer to Gilani.

"I said this is between us, not them."

"Take another step and I kill every one of them right now, soldier boy. None of your heathen lives mean a thing to me. I just need to know what you did with Ramtin."

Suddenly Li's grandmother Ping began shouting at Hamid while pushing her granddaughter behind her. Mac couldn't understand what she was actually saying, but the old woman's tone clearly indicated she was both angry and like Mac, apparently had no fear of Hamid Gilani. Ping Yang had survived during the brutality of rule that was Chairman Mao's China. Tens of thousands were rounded up, imprisoned, or put to death while millions starved under a regime that saw its own population as little more than cattle worthy of sacrifice for what a select group of communist government bureaucrats deemed the greater good.

The eighty-six year old Ping Yang knew Gilani's kind all too well. She had fled a nation ruled by such monsters, only to find another of their kind now standing in her home and threatening her family – a family Ping had brought to America to be free from such threats.

Mac saw the near-rabid willingness to kill in Gilani's eyes. The jihadist intended to shoot Ping dead.

The old woman continued to shout at Gilani as she stood pointing her finger at him repeatedly. Then Mac heard her say something familiar in Mandarin, a phrase she had so recently used to describe him during the reading before dinner. She began repeating that phrase over and over again.

You are the protector.

Mac had forgotten about the gun he taken from Tyrell and left on the table behind him.

Li's grandmother did not forget, and now she was using herself to cause a distraction and give Mac the split second he needed to grab the gun and take Gilani out.

"Shut up old woman!"

Hamid pointed his gun at Li's grandmother. It was the very thing the old woman had wanted – to provide Mac his moment to be their protector.

Mac took a deep breath, focused his mind, and then did what he had for so long done best – deliver.

He lowered himself to half his height as he whirled around and made himself a smaller target in case Gilani's reflexes proved quick enough to fire the first shot. Mac's right hand closed on Tyrell's gun and then he launched himself to the right, again making himself a moving target. As Mac rolled up from the apartment floor, he heard a bullet hit the space he had just vacated.

Hamid Gilani was indeed a fast shot.

Mac completed his roll and came up with his weapon aimed at the terrorist's chest. He quickly pulled the trigger and was greeted by a most unexpected and troubling sound.

Click.

The gun was empty. Tyrell had meant it as a bluff – a bluff that might very well prove deadly for Mac Walker. Gilani continued firing as Mac continued pushing himself forward but the former Navy Seal knew that as fast as he was, no man was faster than a well aimed bullet.

And then something remarkable happened.

Eighty-six year old Ping Yang grabbed onto Gilani and pushed his right arm just enough that the next shot fired a foot above Mac's head. She was doing far more than merely providing a distraction – she was risking her own life to try and save Mac, a man she had just met.

Bless you, darling, I won't let you down.

Mac threw his own gun at Gilani's face, hitting him just above the left eye and momentarily stunning the terrorist who had by then pushed the old woman off of him with an enraged snarl.

Seeing his mother thrown to the floor caused Li's father Charlie to leave his wife and daughter and run toward Gilani, his small hands balled into tight fists prepared to strike. Mac Walker got to Hamid first though, his left foot plunging into Gilani's stomach followed by a hard right-hand jab into the terrorist's nose.

Charlie grabbed onto Hamid's right hand and pulled at the gun, desperately trying to dislodge it. Gilani pulled himself away from the older man and brought the gun toward Mac's head, firing another shot off as he did so. Mac felt the bullet pass by just below his left ear.

He's strong.

Hamid Galina had been fighting his entire adult life – an alpha killer among lesser jihadi warriors. Even as he struggled to overpower Mac, the terrorist remained calm, almost relaxed as he twisted his body away from Mac's so that he might find the space to once again fire a fatal shot.

Mac gripped Hamid's right wrist with his left hand, keeping the weapon away from himself as well as trying to make certain it didn't point toward Li and her family. Charlie had backed away at his daughter's urging, deciding it was now up to Mac to hopefully do what so clearly needed to be done – kill Hamid Gilani.

The two men glared at one another, their faces mere inches apart as they struggled in a strangely tranquil near-silence, the only sounds their heavy breathing as they each strained to overpower the other.

"God is on *my* side, Walker. You cannot defeat me."

Mac's lips pulled back from his teeth as both his arms trembled from the effort of keeping Gilani's arms pinned to his side.

"Your version of God can eat shit and die."

It wasn't Mac Walker's most poetic moment, but it communicated his disregard for the jihadist's religious views simply enough.

Mac's head tilted back and then snapped forward, smashing into the space just above Gilani's nose. Hamid's grip weakened enough to allow Mac to then slam the terrorist's wrist against the wall with enough force the weapon fell to the floor with a loud clunk after which Mac used his left foot to quickly kick the gun to the side.

Hamid Gilani repaid Mac in kind with a devastatingly well placed left knee to Mac's groin. Mac gasped loudly as he felt his grip on Gilani's wrists lessen. Hamid twisted both arms free and then reached behind him to bring out Mac's own gun which he then proceeded to press against the Project Icon operative's skull.

"I told you I would not be defeated."

Gilani attempted to squeeze the trigger but found he was unable to do so. His eyes instantly transformed from reflecting certain victory to panicked confusion at the very same moment Mac's right palm slammed upward with jarring force into the soft underside of the jihadi's chin.

For the second time in half as many days the modified safety feature on Mac's gun had saved him while being held in an enemy's hand. Hamid's knees buckled as he slid downward several inches against the wall while Mac scrambled to regain his sidearm. Before Mac could rip the weapon from Gilani's grasp, Hamid threw the gun across the room, pushed Mac back with his forearms, and then turned to run.

Mac dove forward and wrapped both his hands around Gilani's right ankle, causing the other man to crash to the floor. Hamid spun around like a snapping gator and used his free left foot to smash the heel of his shoe into Mac's mouth, dislodging a tooth. Mac refused to let go, using his knees to push himself forward with the intent to land on top of Gilani and pin him to the floor.

Hamid struck out with his foot for a second time, and then a third, finally forcing Mac to release his grip which allowed Gilani to then scramble down the stairs to the restaurant below. Mac pushed himself upward with a pained grunt and then wobbled from side to side as he attempted to clear his mind from the trauma fog that was the result of the repeated kicks to his face and head, his body not yet having fully recovered from the previous day's beating. He saw the doorway in front of him, heard Gilani's frantic footsteps, and willed his legs to carry him out of the apartment where he saw Hamid looking up at him from the bottom of the stairs.

As Mac teetered to the left, and then fell against the wall on his right while nearly overcome by another wave of dizziness, Gilani grinned, confident of his soon-to-be escape and the resulting likelihood of living to fight another day.

Mac Walker's eyes narrowed as he stared down at that grinning, murderous face. Hamid's grin dissipated as quickly as it had formed. With a loud roar, Mac launched himself down the stairs in a single leap. Gilani froze, unable to comprehend the sight of a man who just seconds earlier appeared nearly unconscious suddenly using his own body as some kind of self-propelled human missile.

Both men cried out in pain as Mac's right shoulder crashed into Hamid's chest. Gilani fell to the floor with Mac on top of him causing the jihadi to scream out in rage and disbelief that Mac had managed to catch him.

Mac in turn had gone silent, though the grim determination in his eyes spoke volumes. He pummeled Gilani's upper chest with the sharp bone of his left elbow and then did the same with his right elbow, followed by a devastating left hook to Hamid's jaw.

Gilani's will continued to match Mac's own though as he jammed the tip of his right thumb into the side of Mac's throat. The pain was instant and considerable, causing Mac to fall off of Hamid and onto the floor as he struggled to fill his lungs with air, his throat feeling as if it was closing up.

Gilani stumbled back onto his feet and began making his way to the exit door but then paused and turned back to face the still gasping Mac Walker. His right foot shot forward, catching the left side of Mac's ribcage with enough force to momentarily lift that side of his body off the ground.

As Mac lay on the floor groaning, his mouth opening and closing like a fish left to die on dry land, Hamid Gilani spit a massive wet ball of blood-drenched phlegm down onto the side of Mac's face. The jihadi leered over Mac for a second more before turning again to limp toward the restaurant's exit.

"Where the hell do you think you're going?"

Gilani didn't want to turn around, his disbelief in Mac Walker's refusal to quit sending a knife-sharp cold shiver of fear down his spine.

He is no man, but a devil!

"I said where the hell do you think you're going?"

Hamid Gilani turned around very slowly, his eyes wide while the corners of his mouth twitched uncontrollably. What he saw glaring back at him did in fact appear to be more devil than man as Mac suddenly ran toward him with murderous intent.

Gilani cried out in terror right before Mac Walker collided with him, his head down and his arms outstretched like some berserker football linebacker hoping to decapitate a doomed quarterback. The force of the tackle sent both men crashing through the restaurant's glass entrance door and onto the sidewalk outside. It wasn't fancy, but it *was* effective. Mac was never one to worry over fighting pretty. Rather, he was one to simply fight hard and most importantly, be the last one standing.

Gilani howled in pain after rolling over onto his back, the result of a shard of glass plunging into the flesh of his lower left shoulder blade. Mac rolled himself back onto Hamid's chest, using his knees to pin the jihadi's arms while he proceeded to pummel Gilani's face with a series of right and left hooks. Each time Mac's fists struck, a grotesque, wet crunching sound echoed against the dark pavement beneath them until finally Gilani's body went limp, his face a mangled remnant of its former self.

Hamid Gilani wasn't yet dead, but he'd certainly seen better days.

Mac gripped Gilani's throat with a scraped and swollen right hand.

"You're gonna tell me the school you plan to attack tomorrow."

Hamid's eyes partly opened as he began his response with nothing more than a blood-soaked grunt.

"No, I don't think so, Walker. What is to be will be and there is nothing you can do to stop it."

Mac tightened his grip on Gilani's neck and then looked up. A large crowd had gathered in the street around him. Li was among them, her expression one of fear and horror as she looked upon Mac Walker's darker nature, fully revealed for all to see. She could not believe the powerful beast with hands torn and bloodied upon the face and body of another human being was the same charming, affable man who sat at her family's dinner table and who she had so recently shared a kiss with.

Mac Walker had seen that look before in other's eyes. His work required an ability to turn off much of his own humanity and allow the monster within to surface, a necessity born of the need to survive where others would perish. It was the only way he knew to make himself formidable enough to defeat the kind of evil that existed in the form of men like Hamid Gilani. Mac also knew that it meant he would likely never enjoy the easy comforts of a more normal life. His would forever be the path less taken, the one that worked to keep others safe. Marriage, family...those were luxuries not compatible with the life he had chosen.

He didn't bother to try and convince Li he was both less and more than the frightening thing she saw before her. It didn't matter. Mac Walker still had a job to do, and he intended to see it done. His eyes reignited their determined fire as they glowered into Gilani's own still defiant orbs.

"You *will* tell me, Hamid. Tell me the school being targeted, and when."

The jihadi's laughter was a barely audible croak, his mouth a bloodied and broken void of torn lips and missing teeth.

"You can't make me tell you anything."

Mac Walker's smile was a whisper of approaching thunder – a warning of a dark and terrible storm to come. He moved his hands slowly up Gilani's face until his thumbs came to rest over each of the jihadi's eyes where they began to apply just a hint of downward pressure.

"We'll see about that, Hamid. Actually that's not *entirely* true. You won't be seeing much of anything."

The gathered Chinatown crowd stood silent even as Hamid Gilani unleashed a piercing barrage of pained screams. The oldest of the former slaves of communist China knew the necessity of what Mac Walker was doing even as the younger among them quickly looked away. Mac was the unstoppable force required to combat the immovable object of humankind gone horribly wrong.

Creatures like Hamid Gilani deserved but one thing in this world.

Death.

EPILOGUE:

Mac Walker looked up to see Ray Tilley walking through the door of the New Orleans Shrimp Shack Pub. Ray was dressed casually in jeans and a blue t-shirt that was not quite large enough to fully hide the hint of a middle-aged paunch that had been sneaking up on the longtime Washington D.C. resident in recent years. It had been the first time Tilley had bothered to make the trip down to the place Mac Walker called home.

He's worried about me.

As for Mac, he appeared to have just stepped out of a Jimmy Buffet video, wearing a white tank top, tan cargo shorts, and a pair of especially tired looking, dark-leather flip flops. A near empty bottle of beer sat in front of him, his third since taking the back of the room booth that allowed him full view of the entrance.

Tilley sat down across from Mac and proceeded to push a manila envelope across the table at him while Mac signaled to the bar for two more beers.

"You look to be well on your way to feeling no pain, Mac. You gonna get that tooth fixed?

Mac took the last sip of his old beer and then grabbed one of the two just arrived new bottles.

"No pain sounds like a plan I can support about now. As for the missing tooth, I'll have it fixed in the next day or two."

Ray's glanced at the envelope that remained unopened in front of Mac.

"It's all there."

Mac took another long sip of beer and then nodded. Ray Tilley had never short-changed him on an assignment payment before.

"I figure it is, so what now?"

Tilley drank from his own beer as his eyes scanned over the pub's dim lit interior. Two large televisions that hung behind the bar cast ever-changing shadows across the low ceilinged room.

"I might have some things lining up for your team in Sudan. Not right away, we're still mapping out the logistics, but it'll be a multi-week job that should pay well. Don't worry about that right now, though. You should just rest up, relax and try and decompress from this last assignment."

Mac began to spin a bottle cap on the table, his eyes lost in its small, circular, metallic blur. Both men looked up at the nearest television screen when a local news reporter introduced a story out of Chicago.

"Chicago PD are reporting three heavily armed men were found shot to death on a sidewalk just a block from the entrance to the city's single largest daycare center. At this time, authorities are not able to confirm if the men intended to attack the daycare. What they have indicated is that all the three men were regular attendees of a Chicago Mosque and were carrying high powered assault rifles, several detonation devices, and dressed in what is being described as military-styled clothing at the time of their deaths. Each man died of a single gunshot wound to the head. It is not yet known at this time who is responsible for the triple murder. Chicago Police are now coordinating with FBI officials in the investigation."

Tilley raised his bottle while looking at Mac, ignoring the follow up news interview that had an unknown Illinois state senator using the killing of the three armed men as an example of why not only Illinois, but all of America, must enact stricter gun control laws.

"Here's to three more dead in the War on Terror."

Mac raised his own beer, brought it to his mouth and proceeded to empty half of it.

"Yeah, just another small little story sure to be ignored by most. Three gone, but a hundred more ready to take their place. I feel like I'm just treading water, Ray. The world's gone dark and I'm getting too damn tired to bother looking for a light. I envy the ones who get to get up everyday living in complete ignorance of what is happening all around them. Must make a full night's sleep a hell of a lot easier."

Both men sat silent, staring down at the well worn, dark wood tabletop in front of them as the news began to report on an Iranian billionaire found guilty of fraud and "crimes against national security" by that Islamic nation's Supreme Leader and chief prosecutor.

Ramtin Armeen was to be put to death within forty-eight hours.

Mac grunted softly and then took another sip from his beer.

"You handed the poor bastard over to the Iranians. That's cold, man. Still, how'd you know they would actually sentence him to death?"

Tilley shook his head.

"We didn't. It was a hunch, one that happened to work out in our favor. How about you tell me how you got Gilani to give up the details of the planned attack on the Chicago daycare?"

Mac glanced at his thumbs while Hamid Gilani's screams reverberated inside his alcohol-numbed mind.

"Guess I just helped him to see the error of his ways."

Ray Tilley had personally witnessed what remained of Gilani's eyes after Mac had conducted a very brief, bloody, and brutal interrogation of him on that Chicago Chinatown street. Just as interesting was the Asian community's repeated assertions to authorities that they had no idea how the dead man whose eyes had been ripped from his skull actually got there or who was responsible for killing him.

Mac's mood suddenly appeared to brighten as he looked around at the pub like someone fondly recalling memories of an old friend.

"Some day I'd like to own a place like this. Nothing fancy, just a little bar where people can close the door behind them and at least for a little while, forget about all the mess going on outside."

Tilley took another sip of beer and tried to picture Mac Walker pouring drinks for people. It was an image that left him openly amused.

"I'm having a hard time seeing you as a bartender, Mac. Working well with the public isn't exactly your strong suit. But in the meantime, here's to America and those who try and keep her safe."

Mac lifted his beer and gently clinked it against Tilley's as he quietly repeated the toast while the world outside remained teetering on the brink and its many evils continued to gather.

"To America."

END.

The sequel to Mac Walker's American Jihad:

MAC WALKER'S BENGHAZI
Mac Walker #3

FREE EXCERPT:

Mac arrived at the back entrance to the cellar five minutes ahead of schedule. He parked his rented white sedan three blocks from the address and then walked, scanning the streets for any signs he was being followed. Having satisfied himself that he wasn't being watched, Mac quickened his pace as he entered the narrow alley that ran directly behind the Mardian building.

The former Navy SEAL saw the posted security detail well before they saw him. They were two large men, each of them no older than forty, dressed in matching navy blue suits with white shirts, well polished dark shoes, and red ties. They were Mardian's men. Tilley didn't hire out for security. He was more than capable of taking care of himself.

The taller of the two men stepped toward Mac as he revealed his right hand holding a simple Glock 21. Mac thought to himself how cheap Mardian must be to have his own security detail armed with such a basic weapon. Not that he had anything against the Glock, it was just so damn obvious – a cliché. Mac had long used his SEAL days SIG MK25 P226 that he had customized years ago to enhance its rapid fire capabilities. Watching the first, and then the second man move toward him, Mac was absolutely confident he could drop both of them before they fired a single shot.

"Sir, need you to stop there please."

Mac held his hands out to his sides, his palms facing the security detail.

"I'm here to see Tilley downstairs - have a 9:30."

The shorter man spoke into his left shirtsleeve while holding a hand to his right ear. Very Secret Service like, but without the actual training. Mac was laughing inside. These two were complete clowns. Clearly from some private security firm that was more interested in having their personnel look like they knew what they were doing, without actually knowing what they were doing. All show. In a real situation, that kind of style over substance gets people killed.

The taller man stood directly in front of Mac and looked him up and down.

"What's your name, sir?"

Mac stared back into the taller man's eyes.

"Walker."

The other member of the security detail nodded to himself as he listened to his ear piece.

"Ok – he's approved. Let him through."

Mac offered both men a thin smile as he walked past them, pulling on the simple and surprisingly heavy red painted metal door that marked the entrance to the cellar. Just inside the doorway was another metal door to the left, and a dimly-lit stairwell that led downward. Mac took the stairs.

Exactly twenty two steps later he faced someone Mac initially believed to be another member of Mardian's security team. This first impression quickly faded though as Mac realized the short, dark skinned, balding man looking back at him with well practiced, casual ease, was a far more capable and dangerous figure than either of the two men outside. This man wore a simple white, short sleeved dress shirt and blue jeans with tennis shoes. He was no more than five foot six, nearly a half foot shorter than Mac, and looked to be not quite sixty, making him some ten years older than Mac Walker.

Whoever the man was – he was a killer.

"Hello, Mr. Walker. My name is Nigel. I need you to leave your sidearm here with me before allowing you inside."

Though the man's appearance suggested Middle Eastern descent, his accent was unmistakably British.

"And who are you with?"

Nigel's eyes glanced to Mac's upper left chest, where his handgun was holstered inside of his light grey and loose fitting military style jacket.

"Your firearm please, Mr. Walker. You can ask further questions once you are inside."

Mac removed his P226 and handed it to Nigel.

"Thank you, Mr. Walker. As you already know, it's right through this door."

Nigel pointed to the entrance into the cellar, a thick, wooden, six panel door that had likely been part of the building's original construction decades earlier. Mac took the few steps to the door and pushed against the heavy, age-darkened brass handle, and walked inside.

The cellar's interior remained as Mac had last seen it. The unadorned walls were painted an off white, the entire twenty by twenty room illuminated by a single bulb that hung from the short ceiling. At the far end of the room was a simple oak desk, behind which sat Stephen Mardian. Tilley occupied a leather bound chair to the right of the desk, while a woman sat in a matching chair on the desk's left.

As he looked at the woman, the normally insistent and prevailing disdain Mac felt any time he saw Mardian, was quickly forgotten. The woman, whoever she might be, was incredibly beautiful. Mac Walker believed such beauty was always deserving of his full attention.

Tilley quickly rose from his seat as Mac entered the room, as did the woman. Mardian remained seated, his eyes hungrily scanning the woman's backside as she turned to face Mac.

"Hello, Mac, I'd like to introduce you to Dasha Al Marri. She works with the United Nations.

The woman nodded her head at Mac, her large dark eyes appearing friendly, though guarded. She wore a long, light grey Gucci skirt, black belt, and matching black turtleneck. Mac didn't know what brand her high heeled shoes were, but they looked expensive. The woman clearly had money, and lots of it.

As Mac extended his right hand to shake hers, he continued to take in her impressive appearance. Likely in her 30's, with very thick dark black hair that she held back in a tight and professional looking bun, and flawless skin that complimented the high cheekbones of her face, Dasha Al Marri was possibly the most beautiful woman Mac had met. Given the three inch heels of her shoes, which made her almost as tall as him, Mac estimated her height to be five foot seven. He quickly noted no rings on her fingers, giving Mac hope that she was single. Mac Walker wasn't interested in a wife, but he was always interested in sharing a good time with a quality woman, and the one who stood in front of him now certainly represented that.

"It is nice to meet you, Mr. Walker. I am looking forward to our doing some business together."

Her accent was similar to Nigel's. She must have spent considerable time in London.

"Nice to meet you as well, Ms. Al Marri."

The woman's face broke into a wide and friendly smile, exposing perfectly proportioned white teeth.

"Please, you can simply call me Dasha."

Mardian had finally stood up from his chair and looked across the desk back at Mac, his deep set eyes and perpetually frowning mouth making him appear as dumb as Mac remembered.

"Hello, Mac."

Mac turned his eyes away from Dasha to give Mardian a brief glance.

"Hey, Steve."

Mac knew how much Mardian hated people calling him by the abbreviated version of his first name. The results, though predictable, remained entertaining.

"That is not my name, Mac – it's Stephen Mardian. You are to call me Mr. Mardian. Am I making myself clear? I believe we've already had this very discussion before."

Mac shrugged back at Mardian.

"Did we? I have lots of discussions, tough to keep track of all of them."

Mardian looked at Tilley, whose eyes were already pleading with Mac to behave himself.

"It's Mr. Mardian."

Mac allowed himself a thin smile as he motioned for Dasha to return to her seat.

"Sure thing, Mr. Mardian - got it."

Dasha and Tilley took their seats as Mac remained standing in between them. All three of them were looking back at Mardian who, after glaring back at Mac, sat down as well.

"Mr. Tilley, would you care to explain the mission parameters to Mac here? I have a 10:30 appointment with a congressman that I intend to keep."

Before Tilley could begin, Mac interrupted, pointing a finger back at Mardian.

"That would be Mr. Walker to you, Mr. Mardian. If we're going to keep this all…professional like. Just saying…"

Mac spotted Dasha out of the corner of his eye trying to repress a smile. Mardian on the other hand, glared back at Mac again before looking over at Tilley, who in turn shifted uncomfortably in his chair.

"Ok, I'll be happy to get us started here, Mr. Mardian. Mac, we need your team on the ground in Libya within seventy-two hours. As you know, with Gaddafi taken out, there's considerable chaos over there, power vacuums. We have the tribal leaders going after the kind of weapons that, well, we don't want those people capable of using that kind of firepower. There's your expected terrorist groups, some former military figures doing business, it all needs to be monitored and the more potentially dangerous elements shut down before it gets too out of hand. That said, we can't be sending in our military to do so. This was a U.N. run operation. At least officially. So---"

Mac interrupted Tilley again.

"So you need us to go in there unofficially. Sounds pretty standard, Ray. Why the face to face with Mardian on this? What else makes this operation different than the others?"

Ray Tilley looked over to Dasha, indicating he wanted her to provide some input. Mac turned his head to the left to look down at her, instantly appreciative of how much better looking she was than either Tilley or Mardian. Taking Tilley's cue, Dasha began to speak.

"What makes this task somewhat different Mr. Walker, are some of the particulars involved. Libya has been dealing in large arms trading for a very long time. Some believe there to be the remnants of nuclear capability. This has become a matter of importance for a great many of us who hope to see Libya's transition be as...smooth and unfettered by violence as possible."

Mac stared down at Dasha, looking past her beauty and trying to see what the motivation behind her involvement really was.

"And just what is your interest in this, Dasha? Who do you represent?"

Dasha met Mac's stare calmly, her hands folding across her slender, crossed legs.

"My position with the United Nations involves a new approach, Mr. Walker. For too long that institution has been viewed as something of a joke among the world's political class. There are those who feel it must...evolve. We must move beyond countless meetings and agendas, and idiotic statements that have no basis in reality, and are ultimately, non-binding. We have been pleased to see this view received rather warmly by the current American administration. Call it a more pro-active approach. We wish to give the United Nations real teeth, so that the world will come to realize if provoked, it can and more importantly *will* bite back."

Inside his head, Mac could hear warning sirens beginning to sound.

"You think the United Nations needs to change, to become what? More powerful, more…militaristic?"

Dasha remained exceptionally composed as she nodded her head.

"Yes, Mr. Walker. Think of it as a new beginning for the organization. A New United Nations, if you will."

Now the warning sirens in Mac's head were on full alert, blaring loudly.

"You want me and my crew to go into Libya to represent this new approach by the United Nations? No way. We work for the American government. I'm former military, we all are. All due respect, Dasha, but I can't stand the U.N., and I'm sure calling it the "New" United Nations won't change that one bit. They've never been nothing but a bunch of pencil pushing bureaucrats always complaining about how shitty America is, or how evil our military is, or that the earth's too cold, or too hot and how if only we didn't drive cars or heat our homes it would make everything all better. Bullshit. No way. I ain't doing the work of the United Nations. Sorry, Tilley you're gonna have to get someone else for this one. Not interested."

Mardian's voice slithered across his desk, dripping venom.

"You already agreed to do the job, Mac. Tilley told me. If you don't want the job, fine. You won't get this job. You won't get *any* job – ever. You'll be doing security at a damn Walmart, you arrogant little asshole!"

Tilley attempted to intervene as he saw Mac's eyes turn dangerous while he stared back at Mardian.

"This is an important operation, Mac. We've agreed to pay you what you asked for, and if this goes well, I know there's going to be a lot more work coming your way. This would be very good for your career. You ain't getting any younger. Time to start saving your pennies, right?"

Mac ignored Tilley, looking back down at Mardian who was beginning to wither under his gaze. Dasha rose from her chair to look at Mac directly.

"Please, Mr. Walker, I have reviewed your file. You are absolutely the right person for this operation. Mr. Mardian is correct. There will be more work available to you after satisfactory completion of the Libyan operation."

Mac's eyebrows rose slightly as he looked away from Dasha and down at Tilley.

"She has access to my file? I thought we were off the books, Tilley? How does someone from the U.N. have access to *my* file? What the hell is going on here?"

"I am connected, Mr. Walker, to more than simply the United Nations. That is my official capacity. Like you, I have what you might like to call, an unofficial capacity as well. Access to your file is not really the issue here. What is at issue is our need to have you take this assignment. Would you consider an additional one hundred thousand dollars in payment, Mr. Walker? Half up front? You and your men could certainly use that kind of money, right?"

Mardian began to object, complaining that Mac was already being paid well for his potential services. This caused Dasha to hold up her hand to Mardian as she ripped through his objection.

"Mr. Mardian, I would like you to simply sit there now and shut up. I don't care for you, and neither does Mr. Walker here and your behavior suggests our feelings are not without merit."

In Washington D.C., it was a very rare thing for anyone to speak to Stephen Mardian as Dasha did at that moment. His personal contact list was a collection of the most influential figures within that city's mighty corridors of power. And yet, much to Mac's amazement, Mardian's eyes lowered and he said nothing, causing Mac to silently wonder who this Dasha really was.

"Now, Mr. Walker, I would like to invite you to my D.C. residence as my personal guest. Let us have dinner and discuss your involvement in this pending operation further. I'm a notorious night owl, so for me a late dinner is the rule rather than the exception. Do you accept?"

For the first time since arriving at the cellar Mac felt nervous. Part of him wanted to tell the woman to go to hell. Another part of him screamed to accept the offer and have dinner with her. It only took a few brief seconds for that other part to overcome his indecision.

"Sure, I'll have dinner with you. Are you cooking?"

Dasha gave her beautiful head a brief shake.

"No Mr. Walker, the meal will have already been prepared. That will leave us more time to talk, and get to know each other better."

The warning sirens in Mac's head were sounding again.

ENTIRE NOVEL NOW AVAILABLE!

"A riveting tale ripped from the headlines that feels far closer to the truth of what really happened in Benghazi than anything the media reports. D.W. Ulsterman is among the best at taking researched facts and blending them with fiction that entertains and informs. Great stuff."

-BIG TEXAS

ALSO AVAILABLE

D.W. Ulsterman's

BENNINGTON P.I. SERIES:

ALL FOUR NOVELS – FOR ONE PRICE!

"FANTASTIC - a Tour de Force!" **-Hercy A. Lord/Literate Lady**

"DW Ulsterman has a hit on his hands in Bennington PI" **-MARLOWE**

"Without a doubt, the best new thrillers on the market." **-David H.**

ABOUT THE AUTHOR:

D.W. Ulsterman lives near his beloved waters with his beautiful wife of 22 years, and their two teenage children, along with two cats and two dogs.

His interests, beyond the always-present task of writing, are music, film, fishing, an often infuriating golf game, respectable BBQ skills, and sampling various wines from around the world. He feels blessed to share his days with the love of his life, and watch their two children grow into the remarkable young adults they have become.

Many of D.W. Ulsterman's personal interests are reflected in his works, including a love of America, classic rock, and the "indelible education that results from experiencing fist to face."

His writings include the bestselling Mac Walker series of books, including the epic tales DOMINATUS and TUMULTUS, as well as the more recent Bennington P.I. series.

This past summer he released his most personal novel to date, The Irish Cowboy.

Like D.W. on Facebook at:
https://www.facebook.com/author.dwulsterman

And follow him on Twitter at:
https://twitter.com/DWUlsterman

Printed in Poland
by Amazon Fulfillment
Poland Sp. z o.o., Wrocław